INJURED HEROES SERIES - BOOK TWO

CROSSROADS OF
DELUSION

DANIELLE M HAAS

Cover created by Deranged Doctors Design.

A Danielle M Haas Publishing Book

Crossroads of Delusion - Injured Pride Series

❀ Created with Vellum

To my husband, Scott Haas, who has shown me for MANY years that falling in love with your best friend means knowing every day will be filled with laughter.

1

Zoe Peyton loosened her death grip from the leather steering wheel of the ancient hatchback that had gotten her through more winters than she could count. Her breath whooshed from her mouth as she pulled into her driveway and put her car in park. She really needed to invest in a heavy-duty truck with four-wheel drive, a thought that occurred to her every time the roads iced over.

A thought that wouldn't do a damn thing for her now that she was home. Her speed was that of a turtle the entire drive down the mountain, where she'd worked much longer than anticipated.

As she pushed open the driver's side door, her phone chirped in her bag. She hurried down the red-brick sidewalk, careful not to fall, and onto the porch of the bungalow nestled between two similar houses in downtown Pine Valley, Tennessee. Not wanting to waste a second in the cold night air, she waited until she swept into her living room to dig through her giant tote bag for her cell phone.

Zoe answered the call, pressing the device between her

ear and shoulder while she shrugged out of her puffy black coat. "Hello?"

"Just checking to make sure you made it home all right." Her best friend, Brooke Mather's, upbeat voice filtered through the phone's speaker.

Zoe smiled, warmed by her friend's concern. "Safe and sound." She kicked out of her tennis shoes and threw her bag on the floor in front of the distressed wooden hutch she used to collect her daily clutter.

"Thanks again for helping prep for breakfast. Chet still isn't ready to hire extra kitchen staff, but I need to find someone soon." Sadness weighed down Brooke's words.

Frowning, Zoe flipped on the lights that chased away the shadows in the cozy room. Unlike most modern homes, walls separated her living room from the kitchen and dining room. She liked the isolation. Keeping one room picked-up for unexpected company was much easier than maintaining an entire house. Hell, most of the time her tiny living room was filled with stuff she didn't have the energy to carry further back into her home. Luckily, she had friends who loved her regardless of her messy tendencies.

Plopping on the light blue couch that she'd purchased second-hand, she sank into the plump cushions and twisted her long legs in a pretzel-like position under her. "I don't mind lending a hand. Lord knows Chet needs help. But I'm exhausted. Teaching sunrise classes at the lodge before opening the yoga studio for the day, then returning to the lodge and closing the evenings out in the kitchen is one hell of a schedule to keep. The hours are starting to get to me."

Brooke sighed. "I get it. I'll start looking for some help, and in the meantime, feel free to cut back here. You can cancel some classes, or I can find someone else to help me get things prepared in the kitchen."

Zoe propped her elbow on the back of the sofa and twirled the end of her ponytail around her index finger. The natural highlights in her deep auburn strands shined in the beams of artificial light from above her. "I don't want to cut the classes. Guests who find peace and comfort in yoga don't need their routine disrupted."

Crossroads Mountain Retreat, the oasis Brooke created for injured law enforcement and veterans in the hills of the Smoky Mountains, had been a lifeline for Zoe when she'd been medically discharged from the army. Yoga had always soothed her, and she'd poured her soul into her moves. She'd found her passion in becoming a yoga instructor and opening her own business.

Her business paid her bills, but her work at the retreat was her way to give back to the men and women who needed some peace in their lives. Something to help them through a struggle she was all too familiar with.

And no one at the lodge was struggling right now more than Chet, the mountain man chef with a big heart and sad eyes. "No way I'm leaving the kitchen stuff to you. We both know you're a disaster with food unless you're eating it. So until Chet is ready for an assistant, I'm all in."

"You're the best," Brooke said. "And to prove that, I'll be at your sunrise yoga class in the morning. Although the cold front that came in today means we'll need to set up inside."

Zoe cringed. "Fine, but let's go to the third floor by the windows. At least we can still enjoy the view."

"Agreed. Good night."

"Night." Zoe disconnected and tossed the phone to her side. Exhaustion weighed her down. She could just slip an afghan from the basket beside the couch and close her eyes, but then she'd never force herself to move into her bedroom. Something she'd regret in the morning when her muscles creaked like old pipes.

On a deep sigh, Zoe slithered to her feet and kept on the lights in the living room as she walked down the dark hallway to the lone bedroom. Coolness coated the wooden floorboards, sending shivers through her body. The thin material of her yoga pants and long-sleeve T-shirt didn't offer much protection against the plummeting temperatures outside.

A subtle creaking sound reached her ears. Goosebumps erupted over her skin, and an uneasy feeling tingled the pit of her stomach. She wrapped her arms around her middle and rubbed cupped palms over them. She should head to the bathroom and brush her teeth, but an eerie sensation had her quickening her pace to her bed and burrowing under the covers.

A silly memory from childhood of her pulling her blankets over her head to hide from imagined monsters made her smile. She wished her Ma was here to remind her that everything was fine, and she had no reason to be afraid.

Unfortunately, Ma's words of comfort from her childhood hadn't prepared her for the horrors of war that now plagued her at night. Horrors that had come from a man she trusted and not foreign soldiers outside of camp.

A soft thud came from the corner of the bedroom, and Zoe's heart sprang into action, beating a frantic pace against her chest. She held her breath, listening for more sounds. The creaks and groans of the century-old house were enough to feed into her wild imagination more often than not.

Another creak tightened her muscles. She shifted to her side to turn on the lamp on her nightstand, and a shadow darted into the room. Fear squeezed her chest. She opened her mouth to scream, and a hand came down heavy on her lips.

A man pointed the tip of a knife against her jawline and leaned close to her ear. "Don't try anything stupid." He climbed on top of her, pinning her to the mattress. Moving the knife, he used the blade to shear off a piece of her hair. He fisted the strands in his hand before jamming the edge of the knife back against her throat.

Panic hitched high in her throat. She lay as still as possible, only flinching at the hot breath beating down on her through the hole of the black mask that hid her attacker's face. Tears stung her eyes, blurring her vision. Her mind slipped into a dark and familiar place—a place she'd escaped to more times than she cared to admit in order to survive.

A place she'd vowed she'd never go to again.

SOFT MUSIC FLOATED from the speakers into Cruz Sawyer's patrol car. He stared out the windshield at the bright lights and bustling patrons of the Chill N' Grill. People in Southern Tennessee weren't used to the frigid temperatures, and they darted across the packed parking lot to get into the warm restaurant. No doubt Wade would have the fire roaring in the giant hearth, probably making the garlicy smell of his famous fried chicken hang even heavier in the air.

The passenger door swung open and his twin brother, Lincoln, plopped onto the seat with a plastic bag on his lap. The scent of garlic and fried goodness filled the car. He shot Cruz a quick grin before shutting the door. "What ya looking at?"

Cruz rolled his eyes as saliva filled his mouth. The food was a welcomed sight, but he didn't want his brother's company. Not tonight. "What are you doing, man?"

Lincoln shrugged, feigned innocence twinkling in his wide blue eyes. Blue eyes that weren't only the same color as Cruz's, but usually mirrored his every emotion. "I know how much you hate missing Wade's fried chicken. I knew you wouldn't want to come in, so I thought I'd bring you some."

Pent-up emotion constricted Cruz's throat at his brother's thoughtfulness. He'd missed having Lincoln around when he'd moved to Pine Valley, but now that Lincoln had found love and moved to town from Nashville, he'd been able to reconnect with the brother he'd missed so much.

But tonight was not about connecting or talking or any other bullshit. Tonight was about being alone and licking old wounds—about remembering the woman he'd loved and lost so many years ago.

"I appreciate the offer," Cruz said on a sigh. "But I don't want to sit here and eat chicken with you right now. I want to wait until my shift is over then go home."

"Trust me, I don't want your company either." Lincoln set the bag on the center console. "Brooke's meeting me. Just wanted to make sure you ate something today. Besides, your shift ended fifteen minutes ago."

Cruz dropped his gaze to the time stamped on the radio. Sure enough, his shift was over. He ran a hand over his head, rubbing his palm in a circle on the top of his skull. "Dude, I wasn't even paying attention to the time."

"Obviously." Lincoln fished inside the bag and grabbed a french fry, popping it into his mouth.

"I thought that was for me," Cruz said, dipping his chin to the bag.

Lincoln grinned. "Call it my delivery fee. You sure you

don't want to eat with me and Brooke? I know she won't mind the company."

Cruz shook his head. "Nah. The last place I want to be is in a crowded bar where people will want to stop for a chat. I just...can't."

Lincoln nodded. "I get it. What about Zoe? You could swing by her place. I ordered plenty of food for like five people." He rested a hand on Cruz's shoulder and squeezed. "You don't have to be alone. Don't have to keep beating yourself up, year after year. Diana wouldn't want that."

The sound of his former fiancé's name was like a dagger straight through his heart. Even five long years after she'd been the innocent victim in a robbery. A robbery he should have stopped before things had gotten out of hand. "Leave the chicken and take your unwanted advice with you." He softened his words with a chuckle, but Lincoln wasn't fooled.

"Done. I'll see you tomorrow." Lincoln stepped into the cold night and hurried toward the front door of the Chill N' Grill.

Cruz rummaged around the bag for a fry and was surprised by how many boxes were packed inside. No way he could eat all this food. Maybe he *could* stop by Zoe's. She understood what today meant to him, and she wouldn't force him to talk about Diana or his feelings or anything else he'd rather leave alone. She was his best friend, other than Lincoln, and just the distraction he needed.

Besides, a cold and empty house was the last place he wanted to be.

With his mind made up, he put the car in gear and headed out of the parking lot. Light flurries sprinkled down from the night sky, and he switched on his windshield wipers. Hopefully the falling snow didn't accumulate. The city was ill equipped to deal with icy roads, and drivers had a habit of panicking as soon as a few flakes fell. The last thing he wanted was to aid the small force in assisting with fender benders and accidents after working a twelve-hour shift.

But being snowed in with Zoe might be nice.

A flash of guilt at his wayward thoughts had him tightening his grip on the steering wheel. He couldn't deny he was attracted to Zoe. Hell, who wouldn't find a tall, beautiful woman with a kind soul and interesting mind attractive? But she was a friend and nothing more. After what happened to Diana, he could never lose his heart to another woman. His line of work was just too dangerous to keep anyone very close. Diana's death had taught him that.

Cruising through the quiet streets of downtown, second thoughts plagued him. Maybe stopping by unannounced with a shit ton of food wasn't a good idea.

Food Zoe would want after putting in so many hours today.

He talked to Zoe daily and understood everything she was doing to help Brooke at the retreat. Making sure she ate dinner was a nice offer between friends. Nothing more. Hell, Lincoln hadn't been making a move when he'd offered the food to Cruz. Why should it be any different to offer the food to Zoe?

Decision firmly made, he pulled into Zoe's driveway and parked behind her car. Before he could change his mind, he scooped up the bag and jogged from the car to the little front stoop. Fisting his hand, he pounded on the turquoise painted door.

No noise came from inside the house. Maybe she'd already gone to bed.

He raised his hand to knock one more time when a

muffled scream from inside reached his ears. Fear pressed against his chest, and he tried to turn the doorknob to get inside.

Locked.

Shit.

He jammed his finger against the doorbell. "Zoe?" He yelled, peering into the slim window that ran the length of the door on both sides. "It's Cruz. Are you all right?"

Sounds of shuffling and banging answered him.

Lifting his leg, he kicked the door. The splintered barrier swung open, and he grabbed his gun. With his weapon trained in front of him, he followed the sounds toward the back of the house. He tiptoed as fast as he could down the narrow hall. One door stood open to the left. He whipped around the corner, making sure no one was in the lone bathroom.

Clear.

The second door to Zoe's bedroom was closed. He evened his breath and silently demanded his stupid pulse to slow down. He needed a level head. Gripping the handle, he pushed open the door and rushed inside.

A sob escaped from Zoe as she sat on the bed with a blanket clutched to her chest. Her long hair hung in sheets around her shoulders, strands falling in front of her face. She sniffed and wiped a hand below her nose.

His heart ripped in two, and he ran to her. "Zoe? What happened? Are you all right?"

She lifted a shaking finger toward the window. "A man. He left through the window. You scared him off." Her teeth chattered, making her trembling words come out between shortened gasps.

He lowered himself to eye level. The moonlight pouring through the window highlighted the large tears coursing over her pale face. Fury ripped through him. Who the hell would attack Zoe in her own bed? Taking a breath, he calmed the adrenaline racing through his body. Flying off in a rage wouldn't help anyone right now.

Focusing on Zoe, he cupped her cheek in his palm as his blood thundered through his veins. "Did he hurt you?"

Shaking her head, she swallowed hard. "Not really. Just a little nick on my neck. And he cut a piece of my hair."

He tilted her head back and blood glistened against the smooth skin along her throat. Sonofabitch. As much as he didn't want to leave her side, he needed to go after whoever the hell had hurt her—*touched* her.

Then, he would kill the bastard.

2

Lingering adrenaline raced up and down Zoe's spine, making her teeth chatter even after the threat on her life had passed hours before. She wrapped the giant throw over her shoulders and sunk deeper into the cushions of her sofa. A million scenarios— all with alternate endings not involving Cruz crashing into her house and rescuing her—flashed through her mind.

As much as it didn't feel like it at the moment, she was lucky. Lucky that nothing more than a cut marred her skin and the threat of the unthinkable never went beyond a clammy hand on her thigh.

"Can I get you anything? Want me to warm your tea?" Brooke sat beside her, her brown eyes wide and full of concern.

Zoe scrunched up her nose. The oversized mug Brooke had made still sat on the coffee table, filled to the top with the lukewarm drink. Her stomach churned. The idea of adding anything to her system made her queasy. "No, thank you. I don't think I could keep anything down."

Frowning, Brooke leaned forward and wrapped her in a hug. "I understand. I'll stop fussing."

Zoe smiled through her tears. Brooke would understand. She'd been through a nightmare of her own—a much scarier one—a few months before. Now, in the middle of the night, Brooke sat with her and waited for Cruz and Lincoln to return, knowing Zoe wouldn't want to be alone.

Straightening, Zoe dashed away the moisture from her face and sniffed up the rest of her emotions. "I just can't believe this happened. How could I have been so stupid as to leave a window unlocked?"

A quick pass through the house had shown the spot where the intruder had gained access. He'd crawled right through a window in the kitchen.

"Don't beat yourself up," Brooke said as she snagged an end of the blanket and tucked it over her lap. "Do you know how many times I've opened a kitchen window to get rid of smoke from the oven, then completely forgot I'd even opened the darn thing?"

"That's different. You're a horrible cook, so burning food isn't uncommon for you." She pumped her knee against Brooke and chuckled, the sound rough and low in her raw throat.

She appreciated Brooke's insight, but Zoe had searched her memory bank and came up empty. The weather was too cold recently to have the windows open, and she'd remember opening one to let out smoke from a burnt meal. Hell, she had barely been home enough to even cook the last few months. How long had that window been left unlocked?

A soft knock sounded on the front door, which she'd kept shut by propping a dining room chair in front of it since Cruz had busted it open.

"You stay. I'll get it." Brooke hopped to her feet and glanced through the window to see who was outside. "Cruz and Lincoln are back." She removed the chair from under the door handle then opened it before stepping to the side to let the two men enter.

Cruz took off the cowboy hat that was as much a part of him as the starched police uniform he wore five days a week. He crushed the hat between his hands and stared at Zoe hard, unrelenting. "We couldn't find him. I'm so sorry."

The defeat in his voice made Zoe want to comfort him the way he'd comforted her when he'd swept into her bedroom and saved her. But her limbs seemed to be made out of rubber, and terror kept her anchored to the plush cushion.

Lincoln stepped up beside Cruz and rested a hand on his shoulder. The sight of the twin brothers next to each other still caught her off guard. Both so striking, identical in so many features, yet Lincoln's longer strands and scruffy face were the direct opposite of Cruz's clean-shaven jaw and close-cropped cut. "Doesn't mean we won't. Officers are still canvassing the area. We might get lucky. Someone could have seen something."

She shuddered, wrapping the blanket even tighter around her body, like a shield against the bastard who'd invaded her privacy and stolen her illusion of safety. "I still can't believe this happened. It doesn't make any sense."

Brooke replaced the chair in front of the now-closed door and returned to her spot on the couch. "Have there been similar crimes in the area?" She secured an arm around Zoe's shoulders and pulled her close.

"I put in some calls but haven't heard much." Cruz shuffled his feet and avoided Zoe's gaze. "Might have to search a little further from town. I'd have heard of any nearby burglaries or attempted rapes..." His voice caught. Covering his mouth, he coughed to hide his anger and frustration. "I'll head into the station and see if I can find any connections."

"Cruz. Look at me." Zoe could feel the guilt that poured off him, and it pulled at her heart strings.

He lifted his chin and met her gaze. Glassiness glazed his eyes, and he tucked in his lips, as if keeping them pressed together would stop him from falling apart.

"You saved me. If you hadn't come over, I don't even want to think about what would have happened. You'll find him and make sure he never does anything like this again. But right now, you need to go home and sleep. Today's been a lot. For all of us."

"She's right, man," Lincoln said. "You need some rest. Even if just a couple hours. We tracked that sonofabitch as far as we could until all signs of him were gone. Nothing more for you to do now."

With his focus still on Zoe, Cruz rubbed the back of his neck. "You can't stay here tonight. Not after I broke open your door."

She winced. She'd call someone first thing in the morning to repair the door, but Cruz was right. No way she could stay here. Hell, even if the door was still attached, the idea of being here alone for the rest of the night didn't sit well with her.

Brooke squeezed her tight. "No problem. You can stay with me."

Zoe laid a hand over her friend's, appreciating the offer. "No offense, but you have one bed you share with Lincoln and a couch I'm too tall to fit on. I'll just stay in one of the employee rooms at the lodge." Brooke made sure to keep sleeping quarters for any employee who needed a place to crash in case the weather got bad, or someone was too tired to head home. Zoe still didn't like the idea of being alone, but it'd be better to be at the lodge with other people down the hall than in her unsecured house.

"No. You'll stay with me." Cruz crushed his hat back on his head. "I have a spare room you can have as long as you like, and I'll be right across the hall. Then neither one of us has to be alone." He offered her a sad smile.

A thrill rushed through her before she could stomp it down. Cruz was offering his home to be a good friend. Not wanting either of them to be alone had nothing to do with the silly butterflies that kept invading her stomach whenever he was near—no way Cruz felt anything like that for her. They'd been friends for years and he'd never given her more than a friendly hug or pat on the back.

Which was probably for the best. She'd been through enough heartbreak to last a lifetime. No need to lose a good friendship over a silly crush that refused to go away. She fixed a smile on her face, determined not to give any more thought to Cruz's simple and logical offer. "That sounds great. Just let me pack a bag."

THE FIRST RAYS of daylight filtered through the thin curtains into Cruz's bedroom. Irritated and exhausted, he threw off his comforter. Sleep had come in fleeting bits and pieces, and there was no need to fool himself into believing he'd get any more rest. Not like he'd expected anything different. Not with emotions so high after mourning Diana all day, followed with the gut punch of finding Zoe sobbing in her bed, narrowly escaping some bastard's nefarious intentions. Images of Diana's lifeless face blended with Zoe's tear-soaked one and twisted his stomach in knots.

Then there was lying in bed, knowing she was right across the damn hall. Images of her had plagued him more than he cared to admit. What had she worn to bed? Was her long, auburn hair in messy tangles around her face while she slept? Was she awake, thinking of him? All questions he had no right to ask. Questions that were so far over the line.

Sighing, he sat and stretched his arms above his head. The earlier he got into the station, the earlier he could start finding answers. Then Zoe could go back home and put this nightmare behind her. Having her gone would stop the ridiculous curiosity that had him tossing and turning in his lonely bed.

The cool air made him shudder, and he pulled on a hoodie and pair of sweatpants before padding out of his room toward the kitchen. The smell of fresh coffee made his stomach growl and had him quickening his pace.

Zoe sat at the kitchen table, fully dressed in her usual black yoga pants and form-fitting long-sleeved shirt. She had her hands wrapped around a giant mug, steam curling into the air. Her faraway stare was focused toward the window above the sink.

"Morning." He smoothed down the back of his hair, even though he'd just gotten it cut. But finding Zoe in his kitchen first thing in the morning threw him off in a way he didn't expect.

In a way that warmed him from the inside out.

She blinked in rapid succession, as if pulling herself from whatever world she'd slipped into. "Good morning. I made coffee. Still fresh."

"Thanks." He headed straight for the cabinet and found his favorite mug, then filled the cup close to the top. Lifting it to his mouth, he blew into the scalding liquid, feeling the need to fuel his veins with caffeine to deal with the day to come. He took a sip and winced. "Strong."

She laughed. "Sorry. I didn't sleep well and needed an extra zip."

Smiling, he joined her at the table. He sat opposite her, needing as much space as possible after his wayward thoughts the night before. "I like it. It's a treat having coffee all ready to go as soon as I'm awake. Even when Lincoln stayed here, the ass always waited for me to make it."

Amusement brightened Zoe's face. "Sounds like he treats Brooke a lot better than he treated you."

"God, I hope so." He laughed then took another sip before setting his mug on the table. "How are you feeling this morning?"

Shrugging, she ran the tip of her index finger around the rim of her mug. "What happened last night seems like a bad dream. Like something that couldn't have really happened to me. Not again. Not here, in this safe little town where everyone's so damn friendly."

He straightened at her words. "Has something like this happened to you before? Has someone hurt you? Someone done anything that'd make you think they'd come after you again?"

She dropped her gaze. "Nothing like that. I just meant after everything I experienced in Iraq, I never thought coming back home would bring danger to my door. I thought all of that was behind me."

Something in her voice didn't sit right with him. He'd known Zoe for years, been good friends for most of that time, and he could read her pretty damn well. And right now, she was holding back. He didn't know why. But as much as he wanted her to confide in him with the truth of her cryptic statement, he didn't want to push her.

He leaned back in his chair, choosing his words carefully. "I know we touched on this last night, but I need to ask you again. Was there anything familiar about the man who attacked you? Did you recognize his voice or something about his posture? His build?" She'd been so shaken, she hadn't provided much insight that could help narrow down a suspect—if one was found.

She wrapped her arms around her middle. "Trust me, I thought about it all night. Tried to pull something from the whole experience that pointed in someone's direction. But it was so dark, and he took me by complete surprise. His face was covered, which muffled his voice."

He assumed she wouldn't have much more to offer this morning. Zoe was smart, and even when in a bad situation, aware of her surroundings. If the tiniest detail that could aid in finding her attacker had stuck out, she'd have mentioned it last night. He took another drink, savoring the bitter taste and the way the steam from his favorite breakfast blend wafted up his nose. The smell was so intoxicating.

Tilting his head to the side, he lowered his mug. "What about a smell?"

Zoe twisted her lips, the faraway look back in her eyes. "His breath was warm on my face. Smelled like...peppermint. Not over the top, but a hint. His clothes were soft, warm. I could feel his body heat coming off in waves." Tears filled her eyes, and she bit into her lip. "This is so frustrating. This man could be out there, hurting someone else for all we know, and all I can offer are two pointless details."

Emotion constricted his throat as a thought came to

him. "Zoe, if he was that warm that means he hadn't just been in the snow."

Zoe raised her brows. "And that's important because?"

Anger pulsed along with the beat of his heart. "That he didn't wait until you were home to break into your house. He'd been inside...waiting for you."

3

The morning shift change was an hour away for officers tucked inside the small brick building that housed the police station. Cruz swept through the doors and threw out the sludge at the bottom of the coffee pot before fixing a fresh batch and heading to his office.

With a steaming cup—his third already for the day—in his hands, he stopped in the doorway and shook his head. Lincoln sat at his desk, face down on a mess of paperwork, soft snores coming from his open mouth. Leave it to Lincoln to insist he go home last night, only to come in himself and work until he literally dropped.

Cruz shouldn't be surprised. Lincoln hadn't lived in Pine Valley long, but he'd forged a close friendship with Zoe, not to mention the fact she was Brooke's best friend. Lincoln would want to find whoever was responsible for breaking into her house almost as much as Cruz did.

Settling into the chair across the desk, Cruz knocked his fist against the wood then leaned back into the seat he'd never actually sat in. Damn, the thing was uncomfortable. He sipped his coffee and watched Lincoln slowly blink then lift his head. His eyes were unfocused for just a beat, confusion as clear as the brown stain marring the wrinkled white t-shirt. "Morning, sunshine."

Lincoln cringed and rolled his head in a large circle while digging his fingers into the side of his neck. "Damnit, I'm going to be sore all day."

"That's what you get for falling asleep at my desk." Cruz hooked an ankle over his knee. "Why are you in my office, anyway?"

"Because my desk isn't in an office yet, and I wanted some privacy."

"I'd want privacy, too, if I slept on the job." Cruz was aware Lincoln wasn't on the clock last night, but he couldn't help the gentle ribbing. "You better not have drooled."

Lincoln glared and flicked a pencil at Cruz.

Laughing, Cruz held up his hands in surrender. "I forgot what an ass you are when you first wake up."

"Just need a minute. And maybe some of that coffee." Lincoln scrubbed a palm over his face.

"Get your shit together, and I'll grab you a cup. And I won't even bitch about you being in my seat if you have some good news to tell me." He set his own disposable cup on the edge of the desk. "Don't even think about touching mine."

Shuffling back into the main, open area of the precinct, he nodded toward a few officers as he made a beeline for the coffee station. He didn't want to waste time with chit chat. Not when Lincoln waited with whatever he'd found on his police station sleepover.

When Lincoln left Nashville, Cruz wasn't sure how he'd settle into small town life. It seemed more than Brooke had chipped away a piece of Lincoln's rough exterior. The big city detective had worked all night, and Cruz couldn't be more grateful. He filled another cup and headed back to his office, using his foot to close the door before easing down in the hard-ass chair he had to remember to replace.

He slid the coffee toward his brother then picked up his own still-hot cup. He leaned back in his seat, trying to keep any anxiety from showing on his face. Not like it would matter. Lincoln always saw every emotion toiling inside him. One of the more annoying aspects of being a twin. "What did you find?"

Lincoln took a long sip as he searched through the papers cluttering the desk. He plucked out a piece of paper and set it on top of the pile. "Like you mentioned last night, any break-ins or attempted rapes in the area would already be on our radar. Nothing like what happened last night to Zoe has been reported."

Cruz wasn't surprised. In small towns, news spread like wildfire, and a man on the loose for breaking and entering would have caught his attention. "How far out did you look? Any similar crimes that could be related?"

"I looked within the county for similar cases." Lincoln tapped on the paper, showing a map of Tennessee, a red circle looped wide around their town. "Found some break-ins when no one was home and nothing went missing that draws suspicion. A woman was mugged, but someone came to her rescue before things got out of a hand. Then there's the rape."

Cruz tightened his fist around the cup and it started to cave in, so he set it down. His pulse roared in his ears. "How far away? Was the perp found?"

"Right over the county line. Man wasn't found or identified."

Cruz snatched up the map and zeroed in on the towns where Lincoln had drawn little red stars. He found the one on the edge of the large circle. Mill Hollow. The town sounded familiar, but he'd never been there before. "Was the woman home?"

Lincoln shook his head. "No, at work after hours. Closing her shop. I talked to a deputy who pulled the night shift, and he gave me the information in the file, but I want to touch base with the detective in charge of the case. See if there are any more similarities."

"Looks like we need to look outside Pine Valley. See if any more cases pop up. I want to talk to the woman, too. If she's willing to discuss what happened." People who experienced traumatic sexual assaults sometimes didn't want to relive those moments with strangers. Hell, he couldn't blame them. But if something she said could help bring this asshole to justice, maybe she'd speak with him.

"I agree. Let's also hit up Zoe's neighbors again. The man who lives next door wasn't home last night, and a few were roused from sleep and confused. They might remember things clearer in the light of day."

Ready to hit the ground running, Cruz hopped to his feet. "You going to be okay? Did you get enough sleep at the desk to give me a few more hours on this?"

Lincoln threw back a gulp of coffee then hissed. "Dude, I got all the sleep I need to be on your side the rest of the damn day. We need to work this case fast and smart."

Cruz agreed but wished he could forget about the badge that meant so much to him. He wanted to be fast and smart and all that shit, but when they found the guy who hurt Zoe, he wished he didn't have to just throw him in a jail cell. For once, he felt the burning urge to dole out his rage and sadness.

Because he had no doubt Zoe's wounded eyes would haunt him for the rest of his life. Begging him to do more.

To make sure this man never hurt another woman again. He just hoped Lincoln was near when that time came so he wouldn't put his fist in the guy's face and ruin the career he'd worked so hard for.

Nervous energy zipped through Zoe. She focused on steadying her breath and relaxing the muscles in her face. The women—and one man—taking her class this morning didn't need to know she was a mess of tangled emotions right now. They had their own issues to deal with.

Brooke tried to convince her to cancel her sunrise class before leaving last night, but Zoe refused. Instead, she'd agreed to move back the class at the retreat by an hour— which unfortunately meant Brooke couldn't attend. No way she'd let her attacker take anything more from her. She'd gone down that road before. Letting pieces of herself slip further and further away, slinking into the shadows, hoping if no one really saw her and what had happened, it'd be easier for her to forget as well.

That hadn't solved anything. All that happened was years of depression and fear and living a life that wasn't really hers.

Never again. Terror might have rested in the pit of her stomach, unwilling to move and wanting to paralyze her, but she'd do her job. Find her peace. Keep moving with one foot in front of the other.

Or in this case, lunging forward with her arms aimed high above her head as she led the small group through their morning meditation. She flowed with seamless energy from pose to pose, keeping her voice low and calm until she brought her hands to prayer and ended the class.

She nodded goodbye and waved. Everyone rolled their mats and headed down the three flights of stairs toward the lobby—or wherever the next part of their day was. Zoe stood tall and stretched, hoping a little time to reflect would help settle her.

A man with a timid grin and close-cropped brown hair that screamed military tucked a blue mat under his arm. "I got to admit, that was tougher than I expected."

She offered him a warm smile. "Not the first time I've heard that. Especially from a man."

Wrinkling his nose, he laughed. "I bet. I'll be honest, I came more for the view. The mountains are spectacular, and seeing them from here, with the windows taking up the entire wall. I figured I could enjoy the sunrise and the thin dusting of snow on the peaks. But after about five minutes I was too worried about pulling a muscle or falling on my ass to see beyond my own toes."

His humor lifted her spirits, along with the notion she'd gotten a newbie to try a class he probably never would have considered outside of the retreat. "Well, I hope you join me again. It gets easier. I promise." She extended a hand. "I'm Zoe, by the way."

He took her hand and gave it a hearty shake. "Dusty. The class *has* to get easier. I don't think it can get much harder."

She shrugged, unwilling to confide that she'd led the class in a host of fairly simple moves. "Nice to meet you, Dusty. Are you heading to breakfast?"

He tilted his head to the side, brow furrowing. The wrinkles that formed at the corners of his eyes made him look distinguished and suggested he was a bit older than her own thirty years. "That depends. Will you be getting some food?"

She reared back, widening her eyes. His answer

unnerved her, but her reaction was based solely on all the pent-up anxiety that hadn't left since she'd noticed the shadow creeping into her room and felt the clammy hand clamping over her mouth. "Me? I...umm...no. I have to get to work. I own a studio downtown." Her new assistant, Tasha, would open the studio this morning, but Zoe had a Mommy and me class she needed to prepare for. One of her favorite classes she wouldn't miss for anything.

Frowning, he held up a hand like a peace offering. "I'm sorry. I hope that wasn't too forward. I just got in yesterday and haven't had a chance to meet anyone here. Become friends or conspirators or whatever you want to call it. I'm not good at being alone. Just wanted some company. Scout's honor."

Forcing her heart rate to slow down, she displayed an understanding look and started toward the stairs. She really did have to get the studio ready for class, but a tightness squeezed the base of her throat. She had a sudden need to get outside and let the cold air sweep across her warm body. "No worries. Everyone here is in the same boat."

He fell into step beside her. "True. All a bunch of cops who probably don't want to be here."

"Cop? I would have thought military." She'd seen his type often in her past life. A charming, handsome man who lowered your walls then swooped in and took what he wanted. Leaving her broken and battered with nowhere to turn.

"Ex-military. Current officer, healing from a gunshot wound. Heard about this place, and figured if it can get me better quicker, might as well give it a try."

Stopping on the second-floor landing, she studied him. "So which is it? You don't want to be here, or you wanted to give it a try?"

He grinned. "Can't it be both?"

She pressed her lips together and continued down the stairs, unsure what to make of him. Not like it mattered. Besides teaching her classes, she didn't interact much with the guests of the retreat. Between her own business and helping Chet and Brooke with the kitchen, she didn't have time for much else.

Especially now. When her world had been flipped upside down for the second time in her life.

The stone hearth that was the center of the lobby came into view, and relief loosened some of the tension in her neck. "I suppose your stay here can be whatever you want it to be, as long as it gives you what you need."

His gaze shot up toward the dark wooden beams that crossed the high, pitched ceiling. "Not sure if it will give me what I need, but it sure is one hell of a place. Looking forward to exploring, and maybe even catching another one of your classes." He lowered his chin and gave her a wink. "See ya around."

She turned and watched him go, his attention making her stomach jittery. Hell, if last night hadn't happened, she'd probably be flirting right back, flattered an attractive man wanted to have a meal with her. Even if it was a buffet breakfast in the retreat's dining room. But this morning, she had way more important things weighing on her mind than giving Dusty another thought.

"Zoe!"

Turning toward the sound of her name, she spotted Brooke hurrying toward her. Her long chestnut ponytail swayed with her, and worry shone bright in her brown eyes. Something in the way her eyebrows dipped low made the hairs on Zoe's arms stand at attention. "Hey. What's going on?"

"Tasha called. Someone broke into your studio. You need to get to the police station. Now."

Dread crushed her windpipe, making it hard to breathe. First the attack at her home and now a break in at the studio? Nightmares from her past blurred with the new, terrifying reality and a fresh wave of fear slammed against her.

No way the man who'd once taken everything from her had stormed back into her life to finish what he'd started, but it sure as hell felt exactly the same.

4

Zoe hurried through the front door of the police station and was immediately buzzed into the main hub of the building. One of the perks of small-town living. She'd known Beau Davis—the young officer manning the gateway to the station—for years, so no reason to rummage through her bag for her identification.

She offered a quick wave then hurried across the crowded room for Cruz's office. A young officer at the coffee station nodded a greeting as she passed by. She smiled then stopped at the open office door. Cruz sat frowning at his desk. Lincoln lingered behind him, arms folded over his broad chest and a scowl on his face. Tasha perched on the edge of the chair across from Cruz.

Zoe plopped her bag on the floor, and three pairs of eyes latched onto her. "What happened?"

Tasha sprang to her feet and threw her arms around Zoe, hugging her tight.

Zoe pulled back, studying her young employee's heart-shaped face. Tears made her blue eyes cloudy. "Are you all right?"

Nodding, Tasha dashed her fingers over her eyes. "I'm fine. Just a little shaken up. Cruz insisted we wait for you here so I didn't have to stand in the cold. I think he just wanted me to sit and calm down."

"Was anyone inside when you got to work?" Zoe slid a hand over Tasha's bicep and squeezed. "Oh God, no one hurt you, did they?" The last thing she'd thought was to give Tasha a heads-up about what happened the previous night. She'd never imagined someone would break into the studio. Her lack of forethought could have put Tasha in direct danger. A punch of guilt pressed against her lungs and turned her anxiety up a few notches.

"I didn't go inside. The lock on the door was busted, but the lights were on. I don't know if they'd been left on or not. I called the police right away and was told not to enter. I came here to wait for you."

Dropping her arms to her sides, Zoe turned toward Cruz. "Has anyone been inside?"

"Dispatch sent an officer to the scene. The studio was empty, and it didn't appear as though anything was out of place. Lincoln and I went through as well." Cruz sighed. "But we need you to take a look around if you're up for it. See if anything was taken. Anything else broken besides the lock."

"Did anyone take a look at the security footage?" She didn't have an alarm system installed—something she told herself she didn't need—but a camera pointed down from the roof.

"We need your permission for that," Lincoln said. "Another thing we can do once we go over there. If you're ready."

Tasha's smooth, alabaster brow furrowed, and she

shifted her weight to one foot, hand planted on her hip. "Why wouldn't she be ready? What else is going on?"

Cruz held Zoe's gaze, dipping his chin.

Sighing, she weighed her options. Small towns were good for quick entry into the police station, but also a breeding ground for gossip. Not that Tasha wasn't trust-worthy, but the small-town lifestyle fostered gossip among close-knit groups of friends. And all it'd take was one more person to be made aware of what happened for the entire town to be buzzing.

But she didn't have a choice. The odds were slim to none that the break-in at the studio wasn't related to the break-in at her house. Tasha needed to be aware of what happened so she could protect herself.

Taking Tasha's hand in her hers, Zoe faced her friend. "A man broke into my house last night and assaulted me."

A shocked gasp blew from Tasha's open mouth. "Oh my God. Are you okay? Did they catch the guy?"

"Not yet, but Cruz and Lincoln are on it." She didn't need a play-by-play account from either of them. They wouldn't rest until they found the man responsible for bringing this terror into her world. "And I'm fine. Cruz scared the guy away before anything happened."

Tasha turned wide, terrified eyes toward the Sawyer brothers. "Do you think it's the same person? That he broke into the studio after he left Zoe's?"

A tiny vein ticked above Cruz's right eye, and he swished his tightened jaw back and forth. "Can't say for sure yet. We need to see the video feed. If we're lucky, we'll see the guy's face and can bust him now. At the very least, there should be a time stamp so we know how things went down."

The thought of seeing the man's face on camera made Zoe's mouth drier than a desert mirage. But as terrifying as the idea was, it had to be done. Without a face—a name—her attacker would just wander the streets, searching for his next victim. She couldn't let that happen. "Then what are we waiting for?"

"You sure?" Cruz asked.

Forcing a thin-lipped smile, she nodded. "Might as well walk over. Tasha, you can go home."

Tasha frowned. "I can come. Really, I want to help."

Gratitude puffed Zoe's chest. "I appreciate the offer, but there's no need for all of us to go. It won't take me long to look around and see if anything was taken. Then we can look through the video footage and be on our way."

Tasha heaved an exaggerated breath. "Fine but call me if you need anything at all."

Zoe tugged on the end of Tasha's long braid, her dark strands so similar to Zoe's own hair color. "Promise."

"I guess I'll head home and crawl back in bed then. See you guys later, and thanks for everything. You know how to keep a girl calm when she's on the verge of a panic attack." She waved, casting a coy smile over her shoulder at Cruz, and waltzed out of the office toward the front doors.

A pinch of jealousy grabbed hold of Zoe, and she studied the subtle blush on Cruz's cheeks.

He shuffled some papers and shot to his feet.

Lincoln chuckled behind his hand. "Smooth, man."

Cruz glared at his brother. "You can stay here while Zoe and I check out the studio. There are plenty more calls to make."

Lincoln gave a salute and sat back down in Cruz's chair.

"You're staying in here?" Cruz rolled his eyes.

"I like your office. Besides," Lincoln waved a palm over the papers stacked high in front of him. "All our notes are already here. Why move them?"

Zoe took a step back and let Cruz pass by to grab his hat and jacket off a hook on the back of his door. Watching the two of them interact made her wish she'd had siblings of her own. Even if they were at each other's throats half the time. She'd spent her childhood alone with her grandparents. A house filled with love, but she'd always yearned for a big, bustling family of her own. Kids and a husband she could heap love and attention on—love and attention she'd never gotten from her own parents after their accident.

"Ready?" Cruz asked.

She stuffed her hands in the pockets of her jacket. "Sure am. See ya soon, Lincoln."

Cruz waited for her to walk out the door then followed, opening the main door to let her outside.

She hunched her shoulders against the harsh bite of the wind. No snow fluttered down from the clear blue sky today, but the air remained cool.

"We can take my cruiser if you want," Cruz said.

"I don't mind the cold. Gives me something else to focus on. Besides, it really is a pretty day." Last night's snow glistened on the undisturbed grass and made the bare trees shimmer under the morning sun.

Silence settled between them as she followed the curve of the sidewalk into the town square. Last month's holly still hung around the gazebo and wreaths decorated the lamp posts. No one lingered on the benches along the walking path, either the cold or the morning hour keeping them inside. Businesses may be open, but most people didn't run errands or make appointments until mid-morning or later.

She could just imagine walking hand-and-hand with Cruz through the center of town, laughing about the leftover Christmas decorations that still decorated the square.

Betting on how long it would take for them to be taken down this year.

But this wasn't one of those silly romance movies about crushes who realized they were in love before the sun set on Christmas Eve. It was January now, and morning—cold as hell, Christmas long past, and Zoe was on her way to investigate her studio for vandalism. Quickening her pace, she hurried past her favorite bakery—not even the sweet smell of fresh pastries was appealing—and stopped in front of the window that looked into her studio.

Yellow crime scene tape stretched across the glass door. She dropped her gaze to the handle. Sure enough, someone had tampered with the lock, rendering it useless. "How is that possible?" She dipped her chin toward the protruding mechanism that would need to be replaced.

"Unfortunately, there's more than one way to pop a lock. Whoever did this has done it before, which gives us more information on him. Something else to search for. Would have been smarter if he'd busted a window or something, didn't show us that he was experienced with break-ins. But that would have increased his chances of being caught."

She glanced up at the camera that angled down toward them, and her heart dropped. "Looks like he made sure he wouldn't be caught going in this way, either."

Cruz followed her gaze. "Sonofabitch. The lens is blackened. Probably spray paint."

"Chances his face was on there were slim anyway. He probably still wore the mask he had on at my house." An image of the masked man had her biting into her thumbnail. She'd never forget the ominous sight. The black material against the darkness of her room, with two holes for him to watch her through. To see her when she couldn't see him. Not even the color of his eyes stood out against the disguise.

"True. We need to take a look anyway. Something could have gotten on camera before it was ruined, and the time stamp is important." Cruz swung around and studied the rooftop of the attached buildings lining the quiet street. "I need to check and see if any of the other businesses have cameras. Someone else might have caught something."

"Good idea. Let's get this over with."

Cruz lifted the piece of tape and opened the door, stepping inside and keeping it wide for her to pass through. "Someone already came in and dusted for prints. There were a lot, so it will be difficult to get any real information, but we might get lucky."

A soft buzz from the overhead lights echoed off the floor. Lingering bits of powder clung to the front desk that separated the small lobby from the rest of the room where classes took place. Wood floors ran the length of the space, the dark mahogany complementing the exposed brick that surrounded the studio.

Zoe tried not to think about the mess. As soon as she was given the go ahead, she'd grab the cleaning supplies from the closet in her office and scrub away all evidence of yet another invasion of her property.

Clearing her throat, she brought her mind back to the matter at hand. "Maybe prints found here will match something from my house last night."

Cruz snatched his hat from his head and rested it on a shelving unit pressed against the wall. "Maybe. But if the prints aren't in the database, all that will prove is it was the same person who broke into both places."

A dull ache pulsed behind Zoe's left eye. She breathed deep, cringing at the leftover dust used to pull the fingerprints floating through streaks of sunlight. "I'll set up the camera footage on the computer in my office." She slipped out of her shoes, then glanced at Cruz with hooked brows until he did the same.

She'd kept the studio space open, allowing room for a bathroom and tiny office behind the back wall. As the only employee of Mountain Serenity Studios until recently, there was no need for another classroom. Now with Tasha on the payroll, she might need to look at expanding.

The narrow hallway was pitch black, and she hesitated.

"You all right?" Cruz asked from behind her.

The warmth of his body hugged her backside. She inhaled deeply, taking in the scent of him—black coffee and subtle hints of pine. His proximity gave her courage, and she flipped on the lights then turned into her office. "Sorry, I just hesitated for no reason."

"No need to apologize. You've been through a lot. But I wouldn't have brought you in here if I didn't think it was safe. Lincoln and I cleared the building after Tasha called."

She nodded then sat on the folding chair she'd never bothered to upgrade and brought the computer to life. While she waited for the programs to load, she opened the side drawer and flipped through the files. "The good news is, it doesn't appear as though anything is missing or broken. I'll take a closer look, but nothing jumps out."

"Do you keep cash here?"

She shook her head. "I take a deposit to the bank every night after I close."

The home screen came into focus, and Cruz braced a hand against the edge of the desk. He leaned over her, flicking his finger toward the keyboard. "Wanna bring up the feed? Or would you rather step out?"

She pursed her lips and glared at the computer. "I think

I got this." Facing her attacker, even if only through a screen, might not exactly be fun, but she wouldn't cower. Wouldn't run. Her fingers flew across the keyboard, and she held her breath as she brought up the footage.

"Can you start it from the time you left last night? Then we can fast forward through it."

"Okay." She did as he asked, watching the familiar scene outside her studio pass by at a humorous speed. Children ran by, their parents walking with limbs pumping at an unnatural rate as they chased after them. A squirrel darting across the street, cars passing while the drivers battled the poor weather.

Then the scene cut to black.

"Stop right there," Cruz leaned even further forward, his cheek almost resting against hers.

She swallowed hard, and her heart thundered in her chest. But she wasn't sure if it was from what she was about to see on the screen or how damn close Cruz was. She backed the video up and played it in real time. The scene froze, and she pressed pause. "Nothing. We can't see anything. He figured out how to black out the camera without getting one freaking shot of his body in the frame."

Cruz tapped the corner of the screen. "But we have a time. He was here last night at 8:42. Ballsy. Close to closing time for most of the shops downtown."

She raised her eyebrows, turning her face to stare at Cruz. "So he came to the studio first?"

Cruz tightened the muscles in his face. "What time do you usually leave the studio?"

"Most nights, between 8:30 and 8:45, but I've been leaving earlier than usual so I can help Brooke out at the lodge."

"He thought he'd find you alone here. Especially when

he walked up, and the lights were still on. When that didn't happen, he went to your house and waited. Zoe, this wasn't a random attack. This guy knows your routine and knows how to find you."

Horror turned her away from Cruz and back toward the black screen. She rewound it again, pressing play and focusing on every single detail in front of her. She needed answers, and she needed them now. She wasn't just the victim of a random break in.

She had a stalker, and he'd proven he was willing to go to great lengths to get to her.

5

Cruz straightened and paced away from Zoe. Her office was small, not leaving him much room— three strides tops before he hit the wall and was forced to turn back around. His pulse quickened and pounded against his throat as this newest information raced through his mind.

A man had broken into Zoe's studio around the time she usually was either still at work, or just getting ready to leave. At a time when businesses on the street were close to closing and people were home to escape the bad weather. When she wasn't there, he'd gone to her house and laid in wait for her return. Then, when she was at her most vulnerable, he attacked.

Sucking in a deep breath through his nose, Cruz anchored his fists on his hips and faced Zoe. An unnaturally white pallor washed all color from her face, and her eyes were huge. As if she were finally seeing this situation for what it really was.

"What am I supposed to do now?" she asked, her voice

shrill and filled with panic. "What all could this person know about me? Why is this happening?"

He shoved a hand through his hair and held on to the very thin leash of professionalism keeping him from flying into a rage. That wouldn't help Zoe, and she was his priority —her safety, her happiness, hell, whatever slim peace of mind he could give her right now. "I need you to think about anyone who's given you weird vibes lately. Some guy who you might have brushed off—no matter how nicely—who can't take a hint. Even someone you've been out with a few times and took it badly when you called things off."

She shrugged, her blank gaze still fixed on the computer screen. "I haven't been on a date in months. Since the disastrous Halloween party I went to with that guy I met online."

He grinned, remembering Zoe busting into the Chill N' Grill wearing the cutest little witch costume. The fact that no one else in the bar was dressed for the holiday hadn't fazed her one bit. She'd plopped down beside him, stolen the beer he'd just ordered, and complained about the asshole who'd blown it with the best woman Cruz knew. "Oh yes. The idiot who made you feel bad that your costume wasn't slutty enough."

She rolled her eyes, but his comment coaxed the side of her mouth to hitch up at the corner. "I mean, come on. I'm not a twenty-something college student. My outfit was completely appropriate. That guy just had a stick up his ass."

The low neckline and high skirt of her costume had been enough to weaken his knees. Not like he'd ever told her that. Zoe's friendship was all he could handle, something this situation only reinforced. His heart dropped at the thought of what he let happen to Diana happening again. Better to keep things strictly platonic. "Agreed, but I want his information. I need to talk to him. Anyone else come to mind?"

"There was a guy this morning at the retreat who wanted me to eat breakfast with him." She twirled the end of her ponytail around her index finger, her gaze fixed on her lap. "He just checked in yesterday, though. Don't think he decided to become obsessed with me and a rapist after one sight."

He blinked, shocked a guest at the retreat had the balls to ask her out. "Does that happen often?"

Lifting her head, she wrinkled her nose. "Not really."

A ridiculous sense of relief had him relaxing his hands then shoving them in his pockets. "Did this guy throw you off at all? Or did his request seem innocent?" This line of questioning had him mentally cringing. He'd rather be breathing down the neck of a criminal at the station than asking Zoe about men who'd shown interest in her.

She locked her lips, and something flashed across her face he couldn't quite pin. "It threw me off, but I was upset about last night and overreacted. He was friendly. Nothing inappropriate. Claimed he just didn't want to be alone and hadn't met anyone else yet."

"You're not telling me something." He narrowed his eyes, annoyed she wouldn't be completely up front. Not when total transparency could save her life.

She shifted in her chair, angling away from him. "The way I reacted to this guy had nothing to do with what happened last night."

He crouched in front of her, not liking the way her energy changed. "Then what?"

"I don't have to talk to you about every single thing in my past in order to catch this guy, okay? I didn't ask you to spill your guts yesterday. I knew you were upset about Diana.

What happened to her isn't your fault. You shut yourself off every year on the anniversary of her death even though you have friends who could help. But that's your cross to bear, and Lord knows I have mine. So just leave it be." She pressed the back of a shaking hand to her forehead and closed her eyes.

Standing, he lifted his palms in front of him. He hated the ache her unwillingness to confide in him, to trust him, caused in his chest. They were friends, nothing more, and she was entitled to her privacy. But he trusted her. Zoe would tell him anything he needed to know, and if she had her secrets, he needed to respect that. "You're right. I'm sorry. Some things aren't my business."

Tears slid over her cheeks, and she wiped them away then opened her eyes. "No. I'm sorry. I shouldn't have snapped. I'm tired and overwhelmed and scared to death. You're just doing your job." She bit the inside of her mouth for a beat. "There are some things that happened in my past. Things I've never told anyone, and what's happening now... it's bringing up a lot of buried emotions."

Needing to touch her, to comfort her in some way, he rested a hand on her shoulder. "I get it. Probably more than you realize. I hate this is happening to you, and that it's bringing other shit up, but I promise you I'll put a stop to it."

Sniffing back tears, she nodded.

Muffled voices sounded from the other room, and Cruz tensed. "Sounds like someone's inside. I'll check it out. You stay here."

Zoe shot to her feet, eyes wide. "No way. I'm coming with you."

He debated arguing, but she was safer with him than sitting alone where he couldn't see her. If whoever broke in had returned, he'd be an idiot to do it in broad daylight and be so damn noisy about it.

Zoe pressed against his back, and they made their way into the narrow hall. He tried not to focus on the feeling of her soft, warm body pressed against his. Damn, he really needed to get a handle on this silly reaction whenever she was close.

A harsh whisper echoed off the high ceiling. Cruz grabbed his gun and pointed it at the ground as he continued forward. Sneakers squeaked against the floor. Maybe the asshole was an idiot after all. Whipping around the corner, he trained his gun in front of him. "Freeze."

ZOE'S HEART jumped into her throat. Someone was *inside* the studio. She hunched her shoulders, making herself as small as possible behind Cruz's broad back.

A man spun around, hands in the air, and fear etched in his slack-jaw and raised brows.

A little boy ran out from behind the man and giggled, delight lighting his face. "Ms. Zoe! I told Uncle Brian you wouldn't cancel class."

Cruz dropped the gun to his side and scowled.

Zoe rested a hand on Cruz's forearm. Her pulse continued to thunder in her veins, even though there was no threat. "They're clients," she whispered in his ear, keeping a bright smile on her face.

Cruz replaced his weapon, but his hard stare and tight jaw stayed in place. He walked toward the man, his pace clipped. "Did you not see the crime scene tape on the door? You can't be in here."

Zoe winced at his harsh tone but understood his frustration.

"I'm so sorry. My nephew was excited for class and ran ahead of me." Brian clamped his hands on Leo's shoulders and pulled him close. "He got inside before I noticed the tape, and I was trying to get him out before he disturbed anything."

Leo's wide brown eyes locked on Cruz. "Was that a real gun?"

A hint of a smile poked through Cruz's gruff expression. "Yes, and this is a real crime scene. You need to leave. Now."

"But what about class?" Leo frowned over his shoulder. "I don't want to go home already."

"Yes, officer. We're leaving now. Again, so sorry." Brian shifted his attention to Zoe. "I hope everything's all right."

"It will be." She didn't want to go into detail, especially in front of the little boy. "Looks like I need to let everyone else know about class." People lingered on the sidewalk and glanced through the window. The Mommy and Me class she loved to teach was scheduled to begin in ten minutes. She'd been so wrapped up in everything else, she'd forgotten to send out a text or even post a note on the door about canceling.

Of course, she thought most people would see the crime scene tape and broken lock and assume they should head home.

"I got this," Cruz said and strode across the room.

His white socks slipping across the gleaming floor took away from his intimidating presence, and she hid a laugh behind her hand.

Cruz opened the door, and his muffled words barely reached her ears over the mumbling crowd and howling wind. But his message was clear as the disappointed adults and their young companions frowned then ventured off. A twinge of guilt burrowed in her chest. She should have planned ahead. Scheduled her classes for another location. Maybe even the retreat. Brooke wouldn't mind.

"Guess we'll see you Wednesday." Brian waved and turned Leo toward the door.

Leo ducked out of his uncle's hold and ran to Zoe, wrapping his little arms around her waist. "Uncle Brian *just* picked me up. If we leave now, he'll take me home."

Zoe smoothed a palm over Leo's back, welcoming the rush of warmth at the sweet hug. She'd always assumed she'd have children of her own by now, but life had taken a different turn. Now she soaked up as much affection as she could with the young yogis who graced her studio with their parents.

She'd never told anyone, but Leo was one of her favorites. He'd be in kindergarten in the fall, which meant cutting out the Mommy and me classes he frequented, first with his mother, and more recently with his uncle.

"Leo, come on. I'll take you to get a doughnut or something. Looks like Ms. Zoe has a lot on her plate, and we don't want to be in the way." Brian extended a hand and wiggled his fingers, a sign for Leo to grab on.

Cruz closed the door and stood beside Brian. He hooked an eyebrow and folded his arms over his chest.

She couldn't help but compare the two men. Cruz with his clean-cut, All-American good looks, and Brian with his shaggy dark hair and brown eyes. Cruz had a few inches on Brian, but not many, and both men were in good shape. But the scruffy whiskers along Brian's jawline gave him a harder edge, which made the name 'Ms. Zoe' sound even more ridiculous coming from his mouth.

Leo hugged her tighter then released his death grip and

tilted up his chin to meet her eye. "Do you want to come?" He grinned wide, showing off the gap left behind after his first tooth had fallen out the week before.

"Leo, come on. Ms. Zoe is busy." With his arm still extended, Brian erased the space between them and grabbed the back of Leo's shirt, playfully pulling him away. "I'm so sorry for the intrusion. We'll get out of your hair."

Leo kept his gaze fixed on her as he back peddled toward the door. He clapped his hands together and kept them in a prayer pose under his chin.

Shaking her head, she couldn't help but chuckle at the boy's theatrics. "Fine. One doughnut. Cruz, do you want to come? We can grab a little mid-morning fuel to help push us through till lunch?" Coffee was the only thing she'd managed to consume this morning, and her stomach growled at the idea of actual food. And she needed just one moment of normalcy or she'd break apart in a million pieces.

"No thanks," Cruz said. "I have work to do."

Tilting her head, she studied him. His vibrant blue eyes never left her as he stood with his feet hip width apart, unwilling to relax his stance. "Do you want me to stay?"

"Nope. Go on. Find me when you're done."

Refusing to roll her eyes at his tone, she took Leo's hand. She needed a distraction right now. She could take a few minutes and get lost in the fantasy of an ordinary morning with friends. One small and impossibly cute. The other handsome and sweet.

6

The smell of melted butter and vanilla hung heavy in the air of Crawley's Confections. Zoe stood in the doorway and breathed in deep, savoring every note of goodness that excited her nostrils. Her mouth watered, and she said a silent prayer of gratitude for little Leo talking her into a quick visit to the bakery two doors down from her studio.

Leo tugged her toward the display case. "What do you want, Ms. Zoe? Glazed are my favorite."

She laughed, enjoying the infectious happiness of the child. She scanned the raised cake stands and pretty plates filled with pastries, croissants, and drool-worthy doughnuts. "I don't have a favorite. They all look so delicious."

"Not to mention how they smell," Brian said, stepping up beside her. "Leo, give Ms. Zoe some space." He leaned to the side, speaking directly into her ear. "He's been a bit sad lately. My sister says he's missing his dad. So thank you for doing this. You always cheer him up."

A familiar ache pulsed inside her. She'd grown up without either of her parents. A tragic car accident when she was young had ripped them away from her, but she'd had the loving arms of her grandparents to fall into. Her own dad might not have chosen to leave the way Leo's father had, but the pain of losing them was the same. "I'm glad I could spare a minute. It'll be nice to catch my breath before cleaning the studio."

"I'm going to take him to wash his hands before he gets them dirty again." Brian guided Leo toward the restroom in the back with a gentle hand between his shoulder blades.

Mrs. Crawley stood behind the counter with her large gray eyes behind her round glasses and a warm smile on her face. "Good morning, Zoe. I hope everything's all right. Everyone's buzzing about how someone broke into your studio. I just don't understand what's wrong with the world these days," she said, clicking her tongue.

Not wanting to spill too many details, Zoe offered a smile of her own. "Doesn't look like anything was taken, and only the lock was busted. Things could have been worse."

"Glad no one got hurt. Now what can I get for you?" She opened the glass door behind the counter and plucked out a piece of parchment paper to gather the goodies.

Zoe bit into her bottom lip as she studied the selection. Most mornings, her breakfast consisted of yogurt and fresh fruit. She tried to keep sweets to a minimum, but if she was going to indulge, she'd make it count. "The chocolate crois-sant with a mocha latte."

Leo bounded back to her side with Brian at his heels. "And I'll take a glazed doughnut, please."

"Can I put them in the same bag?" Mrs. Crawley asked.

"That'd be great. Go ahead and make it two glazed doughnuts. My main man here always makes them look so good." Brian pulled his wallet from the pocket of his jacket.

"Two bottles of water as well and ring up everything together."

Zoe hurried to retrieve a wad of cash from her pants pocket. "You don't have to pay for mine."

Brian rested a hand on hers, halting her motion and cranking up her body heat by about ten degrees. "I'm not. He is." He hiked a thumb in Leo's direction. "Dude's got to learn if he asks a pretty woman out for a doughnut, he's got to pick up the tab."

She slipped her hand from under his and swallowed hard. The unwanted touch had her mouth going dry.

Leo giggled.

She took a step away, needing to put some space between them. Brian was a nice guy, but she didn't know him very well. She didn't want to give him the wrong idea about why she'd agreed to join them. "Leo, should we pick out a seat while your uncle pays?"

"Sure!" Leo hiked up onto his tiptoes, grabbed the bag Mrs. Crawley offered, then took off toward the limited seating scattered around the room.

Brian chuckled and humor danced in his dark eyes. "The kid never slows down. Go ahead and sit. I'll be right there."

She followed Leo to a bistro table situated in front of the large picture window, the name of the bakery scrawled across the glass in pretty gold letters. He pulled over a third chair and sat at the seat in the middle. "Sit by me, Ms. Zoe."

A chill swept over her, and she wished Leo had picked the table nestled in the corner. Sitting in front of the window felt like being center stage, an easy target for whoever was after her. She scanned the scene in front of her. A few pedestrians strolled along the sidewalk, popping in and out of the bustling businesses downtown. The bare branches of the trees swayed with the wind. Nothing stood out. Nothing screamed for her attention. But she couldn't stop the feeling crawling up the back of her neck that someone *was* there. Watching and waiting.

"Ms. Zoe?"

Blinking herself back to the moment, she pulled out the chair and sat. "Sorry, Leo. I zoned out for a second."

"I do that at preschool. Ms. Anne gets mad at me. She says I can't do that in kindergarten." He said his 'r' in the cute way only a child missing a tooth could.

Zoe ruffled his dark flop of hair. "I wouldn't worry about that now."

Brian shimmied to the side to maneuver around the small, circular table and took the empty seat beside her. "Don't worry about what?" Leaning forward, he placed a napkin on the table in front of Leo then opened a bottle of water before retwisting the cap and handing the bottle to Leo.

"Kindergarten." Zoe plucked her croissant from the bag. "That's months away."

"I'm in denial he's going. No way he's old enough. Leo, you can't be older than, what? Three?" Keeping his very serious expression on Leo, Brian bit into his doughnut.

Leo wrinkled his nose then wiped a smear of glaze from his chin with the back of his hand. "I'm five, Uncle Brian. You know that."

"Oh, that's right. Your mom did tell me. But that silly sister of mine teases sometimes. I can't always believe her."

Appreciating the goofy banter, Zoe tore off a piece of her croissant and popped it in her mouth. The buttery pastry filled with warm, gooey chocolate was pure heaven. "I forgot how much I love these. Thank you for this. Just the pick me up I needed after a rough morning."

"I'm sorry about my little criminal busting into the studio," Brian said. "I hope he didn't disturb anything."

"I didn't touch anything, Ms. Zoe." Leo's lip trembled.

She dusted off the powder sugar from her hand then rested a palm over Leo's knuckles. "You didn't hurt anything. Promise. All that's left for me to do is head back there and get the place cleaned up."

Leo brightened. "So we can have class on Wednesday?"

"Absolutely."

"Good. I can't keep bringing him for sweets or his mom will kill me. Not to mention these outings are supposed to help drop weight, not put it on." Brian leaned back and patted his stomach.

She raised her brows, suppressing a grin. She might not know Brian well, but she'd seen the way his shirts molded against his body when he did the moves with Leo during class. Extra weight wasn't something he needed to worry about. If she had to guess, nothing but chiseled abs hid underneath the fleece jacket he wore.

Her gaze drifted to the washboard stomach where her mind had wandered. Yoga with a five-year-old couldn't be all he did to stay in shape.

"Zoe?"

"Hmm?" She snapped up her gaze and met the amusement dancing in his eyes. Humiliation burned her cheeks.

He bit into his doughnut, grinning around a mouthful of glaze.

She took a sip of her latte and counted the seconds before it'd be appropriate to excuse herself. This was a mistake. She wasn't in the right frame of mind for anything, let alone an innocent conversation with an attractive man and adorable child. They were a dangerous combination— disarming on her best day.

Cruz walked past the window, stopping to stare at a spot above the glass, before hurrying inside. He caught her gaze and hesitated, a flash of emotion skittering across his face. She couldn't quite figure it out, but something about the way he dropped his shoulders and ducked his chin constricted her chest. He was making it hard to catch a breath.

No matter how enchanting the uncle and nephew duo beside her was, they had nothing on the illogical pull Cruz had on her—like a magnet drawing her close. Fighting the attraction was exhausting, but something she had to do. She couldn't open her heart all the way to anyone ever again, and Cruz deserved more than that. Even if he didn't realize it. One day, he'd want a happy life with a woman he loved. And the devastating truth was, she could never be that woman.

IRRITATION CRAWLED over Cruz like an army of fire ants. Seeing Zoe laughing and carefree with another man took his bad mood and made it ten times worse. How could she run off with some guy when she'd just found out she had a stalker?

Okay, so she hadn't *run off*, and the kid was the one who'd asked her to tag along. Cruz had also kept her in his sights as she sat in the window and munched away on her damn dessert, unaware of his eyes on her. But even if he was capable of watching over her while also checking the street for more cameras, it didn't mean he had to like it.

The little boy—Zoe had called him Leo—waved his arm in a large, sweeping motion. As much as the kid amused him, Cruz had no desire to join the happy trio. But he couldn't ignore them. Not when Leo's face lit up, and Zoe stared at him with those rounded eyes. He held up an index finger to indicate he'd be over in a minute, then made his way to the counter to speak with Mrs. Crawley.

"Hello, Cruz." Mrs. Crawley propped an elbow on the glass counter and rested her chin in her palm. Concern made the crow's feet around her eyes more pronounced. "Don't usually see you until the afternoon for your midday treat. Need something to get you through the morning?"

He scanned the tempting sweets but didn't need any more distractions. His mind was already too focused on Zoe and her yoga buddy when it should be on the case at hand. "I need something, but I'm afraid none of your tasty treats. Can I take a look at your security footage from last night?"

Mrs. Crawley dropped her casual pose and frowned. "Of course. But why?"

"The camera outside the bakery has a good angle of the sidewalk. I might catch a glimpse of the person responsible for breaking into Zoe's studio. If not in the act of entering itself, at least coming or going."

"Becky's using the computer to figure out inventory right now. Let me go ask her to stop what she's doing so I can tinker with the system and get what you need."

He tried his hardest not to react to the word tinker and failed when a chuckle rose from his throat. "I don't want to get in anyone's way. Can you just give me the tape? I'll run over to Zoe's and watch it real quick then bring it right back over. Then you don't have to...tinker." He smiled at the word, the sound odd coming from his mouth.

Mrs. Crawley chuckled and slapped a hand through the air. "Stop that teasing. Give me a second." She disappeared behind the wall that boasted the daily specials and menu.

No longer having an excuse to avoid Zoe and her

friends, he ambled toward the table. "How are the doughnuts?"

"So yummy! Ya want one?" Leo asked, making a wide circle around his lips with his tongue.

"No thanks. I just popped in for a minute and have to get back to the studio."

Zoe straightened. "Did you find anything?"

Cruz flicked his gaze around the table before settling it on Zoe. "Not sure." He couldn't exactly confide in her with strangers around. Even if one was only five.

She narrowed her eyes, scrutinizing him, and he tightened every muscle in his body so he wouldn't squirm.

"I can grab you something to go," Brian said. "Always want to support the local police. Least I can do."

"You're not local," Leo said, laughing.

Brian rolled his eyes. "Please excuse my nephew. He takes everything very literally."

Leo scrunched up his nose. "What's that mean?"

"Cruz. I have that footage for you." Mrs. Crawley waved the tape.

"You're looking at her security footage? Why didn't you say so? I want to see it." Zoe gathered her brown to-go cup and offered an apologetic smile. "Sorry to cut this short, but I'll see you both at Wednesday's class. Thanks again for breakfast." Leaving her half-eaten croissant on the table, she jumped to her feet.

A sense of victory lifted Cruz's spirits as Brian frowned, but Cruz offered a small wave.

"Bye, Zoe," Leo said, his voice muffled by the doughnut he'd just shoved in his mouth.

Cruz gave a curt nod then retrieved the tape from Mrs. Crawley. He led Zoe out of the bakery and back to her studio.

"I'll take that," Zoe said, grabbing the tape once they stepped foot in her office. She sat down in the chair she'd been in earlier and queued the footage with the same efficiency as before. "I helped Mrs. Crawley pick out her security system a few years ago. We have the same cameras."

Unable to stop the strange desire to be near her, he grabbed a step stool from the corner and positioned it beside her. He lowered himself onto it, testing the weight limit as he eased himself down. "Start the video for about fifteen minutes before your studio was broken into. We might catch him before he breaks in."

Zoe pressed a few buttons on the keyboard and sped through the video until satisfied with the time on the screen, then played it at a slightly faster pace.

Cruz studied every inch of the footage. A shadow from the opposite side of the studio emerged. "Stop." He pointed toward the slim form, barely visible from the awkward angle. "That'd be to the left of your door, right?"

Squinting, Zoe leaned forward. "I think so. And it's about the same time my camera was blacked out. He must have stayed to the side so my camera didn't pick him up."

"So much for catching something before he broke in. Play it through."

The video began again. The figure shifted, his side now visible.

"He's wearing black, just like at my house." Her voice was hollow, her body tense. "And he's wearing gloves."

"So much for fingerprints." Damnit. He'd hoped to find good news on the security cameras. Not another stumbling block that'd make finding this bastard more difficult. "What does he have in his hand? Keys?"

Zoe inched her face so close to the screen, her nose almost pressed against it. "Maybe? It's hard to tell, and I don't have the ability to zoom in here. Can you manipulate the footage at the station?"

"It's worth a try. I need to get permission from Mrs. Crawley first." On screen, the door to the studio swung open and the man slipped inside. A few minutes passed before the man appeared again. He shut the door, hunched his shoulders forward, and proceeded down the sidewalk. Passing right by the bakery. The hood from his sweatshirt was pulled over his head and his chin turned down, keeping his face off camera. "Why did he approach the studio from one side, then leave in the opposite direction?"

Sighing, Zoe leaned back in the chair and squeezed the bridge of her nose. "Did anyone else on the street have a camera he could have passed?"

"Nope. Just you and Mrs. Crawley." He shook his head, for once hating the small-town charm that coaxed its citizens into a sense of security. Pine Valley might be a safe place to live, but bad stuff happened everywhere and people needed to be prepared.

Hell, Zoe was more prepared than most. That hadn't stopped some creep from blowing up her life. He caught her eye, and she hooked a strand of hair around her finger, as if needing to find anything to fix her nervous energy on.

The asshole might have snuck through their defenses once, but Cruz wouldn't let it happen again.

7

The folding chair in Zoe's office made Cruz yearn for his soft leather desk chair back at the station. But that wasn't an option right now. Not when Zoe needed to clean her studio, and he refused to leave her feeling vulnerable and alone.

After they'd gotten permission from Mrs. Crawley to take her security tape to the station, Zoe had come with him to drop it off to the IT guy. Now he had calls to make. Calls he could make anywhere, so he'd opted for the tiny desk with Zoe's signature clutter everywhere—really, who kept a vintage snow globe on their desk next to a fake planter that held flower-shaped pens? A choice Zoe had protested, claiming she could be alone in the middle of the day.

Although Cruz had noticed the relief she couldn't hide. Relief that had relaxed the tightened planes of her face when he refused to budge on his decision.

Now, harsh scents of disinfectant mixed with a hint of lemon as Zoe scrubbed away whatever invisible traces the burglar had brought into her sanctuary. As soon as he finished with his calls, he'd go out and help.

He'd left a message with the woman Lincoln had discovered had been attacked at work, after speaking with the officer in charge of her case. He had one more call to make before he touched base with Lincoln, who opted to head out to the retreat to speak with the man who'd wanted to eat breakfast with Zoe after class.

Skimming the list of questions he had for Zoe's one-time date, he dialed the number then pressed the speaker button before setting his phone on the desk.

"Thanks for calling Mike's Motors, how can I help you?" A gruff, scratchy voice threw out the question as though he didn't really want to help a damn soul.

"I'm looking for Mike Bradford." He wouldn't announce who he was or what he needed until he got the other man on the phone.

"You got him. Need to schedule an appointment?" The sound of computer keys being hit clicked through the speaker.

"No appointment. I'm Officer Cruz Sawyer, and I need to talk to you about Zoe Peyton."

"Who?"

Anger tightened his grip on his pencil. Zoe might have only gone on one date with this idiot, but a woman like her should never be forgotten. "You met on a dating app in October of last year. Went on a date to a Halloween party."

Mike snorted. "Oh, her. What about her?"

Cruz fought to reign in his temper. "Have you attempted to contact her since the night you took her to the Halloween party?"

"Why would I do that? She had no sense of humor. Left *me* at the party. Can you believe that?"

Yes, actually Cruz could believe it based on what an ass

the guy sounded like. "So you haven't seen her or spoken with her since October?"

"Hell, no, man. Why waste time on a woman like that, ya know? Plenty of other ladies willing to chomp at this bit."

Cruz cringed at the analogy. Did this guy realize what a dipshit he was? "Thanks for your time."

"That's it? All you need?" Skepticism dripped over Mike's words.

Cruz ran a thin line through the questions he'd prepared, unsurprised to have gotten nowhere with this phone call. "Yep. If I can think of anything else I need to know, I'll reach out." He disconnected then threw down the pencil. Mike Bradford was just as charming as Zoe had described. Cruz still needed to take a look at the guy's background, but as of now, he was low on the limited list of suspects. He called Lincoln, hoping his brother had more luck at the retreat.

Lincoln answered after one ring. "Hey, man. Was just about to call you. Did you get any information we can use?"

Leaning back, Cruz scratched the top of his head before dropping his arm, letting it dangle at his side. "Not really. I left a voicemail for the victim you uncovered, and the man Zoe had a date with was full of crap."

"Like he lied on the phone?"

"No, like most of his day is spent spewing out his own bullshit. Total asshole. I want to see if he has a criminal history, but my gut says he's not the one we're looking for."

"Sounds pleasant. I talked to Brooke about this Dusty dude who approached Zoe before I sought him out," Lincoln said.

Zoe poked her head around the corner, stealing his attention. Her hair hung over her tilted shoulder, the rest of her body hidden on the other side of the doorframe. "I'm going to mop. Stay in here until the floors are dry." She disappeared as quickly as she'd appeared.

"Dude! You there?"

Lincoln's annoyed pitch brought Cruz back to the conversation. "Sorry. What about Dusty?"

"Guy's name is Dusty Sommerfield. Was given a medical discharge from the army, and now he's at the retreat because of an injury while in the line of duty. Brooke said his record is clean and tidy, but of course it would be or she wouldn't have allowed him to be a guest."

"Clean and tidy could mean he knows how to not get caught. Did you talk to him?"

"I caught him right before he was heading outside for some outdoor meditation or something. He said he'd talk to me after, no problem. I'm just waiting around until he's free."

Cruz rolled his eyes. "I'm sure that's a hardship. Tell Brooke I said hi." If given the choice, Lincoln stayed glued to his fiancé's side. Not like Cruz blamed him. The two had been through hell together, coming out the other end stronger and ready to profess their love. A true *Titanic* love story. Without the drowning, of course. Now they soaked up as much pre-wedding bliss as possible. If he wasn't so damn happy for his brother, he'd be disgusted.

Lincoln laughed. "Shut up, man."

"Zoe's finishing cleaning the studio. She wanted it ready to open tomorrow. The locksmith will be here soon, then he'll head out to Zoe's house to see if he can fix the busted door as well as put on better locks." Cruz flipped the notepad closed then stretched onto his feet. "Once I know the situation there, I'll knock on some neighbors' doors."

"Sounds good. I'll be in touch."

Cruz disconnected the call then pocketed his phone.

Leaning into the hall, he scanned the gleaming hardwood floors. Glistening streaks reflected in the light, clueing him in to the still-wet floors. "Zoe?" He chuckled at the weariness of his own voice. He'd been a police officer in the city of Nashville for years before coming to Pine Valley and had encountered some of the city's most dangerous criminals. But none of them put the fear of God in him like a woman who'd be pissed he mucked up her clean floors.

He shook his head and slunk back into the office. Zoe had gotten under his skin in a way no other woman had since Diana. He just hoped he could protect Zoe. If he failed, and she was hurt because of it, he'd never bounce back. Whether he admitted she had his heart or not didn't matter. All that mattered was Zoe's safety. Which told him everything there was to know about his true feelings.

But what was he going to do about it?

BEADS OF SWEAT dotted Zoe's hairline. She wiped them away with the back of her wrist and leaned on the handle of her mop. The floors shined, and not one streak or speck of dust marred the mirrors on the back wall. Hell, she'd even dragged out every mat and scrubbed them down. The place hadn't been this clean since she'd first bought it.

If only she could scour away the lingering sense of ickiness the intruder left behind when he'd broken into her place of business with the intent to corner and rape her.

She shuddered, and for the hundredth time tried to drag out any memories she may have suppressed. Any clues that could point a glowing, neon sign in the direction of the person who would want to do such a heinous thing to her. Defeat slumped her shoulders. Nothing sprang to mind. No new distinguishing characteristics or anything familiar about the man who'd pinned her down and grazed the tip of a knife against her jaw came to mind.

The scratch throbbed, and she ran the pad of her finger against the superficial wound. A sick term for an injury that was anything but small and inconsequential.

A sharp rap sounded on the door, and she jumped before turning toward the glass. She breathed a sigh of relief at the sight of Bobby in his familiar overalls and red, stained baseball hat. After telling the local handyman about what had happened, he'd agreed to meet her at the studio as soon as he could.

"Someone here?" Cruz called from the office, his head craned around the doorframe. "Are the floors dry?"

She couldn't help but laugh at his worried tone. "Bobby's here to fix the locks, and yes, the floors are dry."

Cruz darted into the hall and approached. His pronounced frown told her that he had more information he didn't want to tell her.

"You all right?"

He shook his head and offered a quick squeeze to her shoulder before he passed by on his way to the door. "I'll tell you about it in a second. I want to talk to Bobby."

She followed, needing to speak with the retired handyman who never actually stopped working. Bobby was a staple in Pine Valley, puttering around town, fixing all the odds and ends that broke in homes and businesses. He was a wealth of knowledge who hated being bored—something he realized after he sold his hardware store to his nephew a few years prior. A personality trait that kept him working well into his seventies and annoyed his wife to no end.

Cruz yanked on the handle and a whoosh of cold air flowed into the studio.

Zoe rubbed the gooseflesh from her arms. "Come on in, Bobby."

Bobby gripped the bill of his red ball cap, sweeping it off his head and jamming it into the back pocket of his denim overalls—his daily clothing choice was another town staple. "Thanks, Zoe. I got here as soon as I could. Had a job scheduled first thing this morning I couldn't let sit."

"I appreciate you squeezing me in. I don't want to leave here until proper locks are installed."

"Don't blame you one bit." Bobby hoisted a rusted toolbox in the air. "Brought my best stuff. I can get the lock in real quick. The door at your place might be more of an issue if it's as busted as you said."

"Mind if I take a look at the lock?" Cruz asked, peering in the box. "She also needs a new camera installed, but that can wait until tomorrow if you don't have one available."

Bobby set his toolbox at his feet and fished out a white, cardboard box with the picture of a lock and a smiling woman on the front. "Top of the line. Deadbolt and a new handle for the door."

Cruz took the box and studied it, nodding along as he mouthed the words he read. "Looks good. Thanks, Bobby."

"I'll need to order a camera, unless Zoe has one of those fancy new ones. You know, the ones where the video shows up on your phone. Those are easy as pie to install and might give you a little more peace of mind, Zoe."

"I like the idea of seeing who's at my door—or at the door of the studio—on my phone," she said. "But I want one on the building as well."

"You got it. Give me a few minutes to get this installed then we can head to your place." Bobby shuffled toward the door and rummaged around in his toolbox until he found what he needed.

"While he works, we need to talk," Cruz said. "How about I go next door and grab a couple sandwiches? I don't know about you, but I'm starving."

As if on cue, her stomach growled. Afternoon had come a few hours ago, and the bites of the croissant she'd eaten earlier hadn't stayed with her. "Good idea."

"I'll grab them while you finish up in here. Turkey on wheat?"

She nodded, and bit back a grin. Not surprised that he'd know exactly what to order for her. They'd shared enough meals over the last few years for him to guess her order. "And a bottle of water."

"I'll be right back."

She watched him slide past Bobby, displaying an easy smile on his handsome face for the older man. Cruz hurried toward the market. Sighing, she tore her gaze away from his familiar frame and busied herself putting away all the cleaning supplies she'd dragged out. By the time Cruz returned with their late lunch, she'd set up a place for them to eat at the two chairs nestled in the tiny waiting area in front of the lobby's desk. She didn't want to be back in the office, out of sight of everything going on around her.

Cruz unwrapped his sandwich then laid it on his lap, fixing her with a concerned stare. "While you were cleaning, I ran another search for reported rapes in the area. Lincoln found a case in the next town over. I pushed the search perimeters further out, over to the surrounding counties, and the cases increase at an alarming rate."

"How many?" Zoe was afraid to ask, but she had to know.

"Six."

The hunger from earlier vanished, and Zoe set her

unwrapped food on the little table. "That's awful. Has anyone been arrested?"

Taking a bite of what looked like ham and cheese, Cruz shook his head.

Her stomach dropped. "Do you think any of these cases could be related? I mean, why would a man who lives in another county come here and attack me?"

"Could be new to town, or even a guest at the retreat. Someone who has a penchant for this type of crime wouldn't want to get caught and would need to move around, not stay in one place too long." He wiped his mouth with a napkin then took a swig of water. "I need to pull more data and look for patterns. With any luck, something will jump out and lead us to some answers."

"Hopefully." Pulling her legs under her, she curled into a ball. "Those poor women."

"They'll want to find this guy as much as we do."

"Sorry to interrupt, but I'm all done here," Bobby said. "Ready to head to your house, Zoe?"

Cruz gestured toward her untouched food. "Take that with us. You can eat in the car. Even if you don't feel hungry." He raised his brows as he stood, reading her thoughts.

She huffed out a breath. "Fine." For Cruz's benefit, she'd manage a few bites on the quick trip then throw the rest of the turkey in the trash. The idea of other women experiencing a similar fear—and worse, the pain and terror she'd escaped—formed a lead ball of anxiety and sadness in the pit of her stomach.

Rising, she stuffed her feet in her sneakers by the door and threaded her arms through her jacket. She pocketed the bottle of water and scooped up the sandwich. "Ready?"

With his mouth full of the rest of his lunch, Cruz

nodded. He swallowed then headed for the door. "We'll meet you at Zoe's. We have to walk to my car at the station."

"I'd give you folks a ride, but my truck is packed. Wouldn't be enough room for both of you." Bobby handed Zoe a set of keys. "You'll need these. See ya in a few."

Zoe waited for Bobby and Cruz to exit then locked up before falling into step beside Cruz. Silence hung between them. Her mind was unable to concentrate on anything except her conversation with Cruz. On the women who'd been victimized and the man who'd taken so much from them. "Do you think the same man is responsible for all the different cases?"

Waiting for a duo of gray-haired women to pass by, Cruz said, "Can't be sure. At least not yet. But the chances of multiple rapists in such a small area seems a little far-fetched."

A shiver raced down her back that had nothing to do with the cold temperatures. "If it's the same man, how did he pick his victims? Were his choices random, or did he make some connection between everyone?"

"Good question, and one I plan to find an answer to. I was working on my phone, so the information I gathered was limited. I need to speak with the detectives in charge of all these cases, the women themselves if they'll talk to me." He turned the corner toward the police station, where he'd parked his car on the street across from the brick building.

"Maybe the women would feel safer talking to me. Maybe if we spoke, we might figure out some connection drawing this sicko to us." She quickened her pace, the rush of wind barreling toward her stealing her breath.

She reached the passenger side of the car, and Cruz hurried to grab the handle to open her door. She offered him an appreciative smile before settling onto the soft leather. A piece of paper on the windshield caught her attention, and she pointed to it. "What's that?"

Shrugging, Cruz shut the door and rounded the car, freeing the paper from under the wiper blade. His eyes widened, and he locked his jaw. He cast a quick glance around him then yanked open the driver's side door and thrust the paper inside for her to see. "Don't touch it."

Bright red letters scrawled over the light blue paper.

Stay away from her. She's mine.

8

With twilight behind Zoe and a days' worth of questions and emotions dragging her down, she curled into the corner of Cruz's soft couch and struggled to keep her eyes open. Fear had kept her glued to Cruz's side the entire time they'd spent at the police station, pouring through more security footage. Because Cruz had arrived to work early and been forced to park on the street across from the building, his cruiser was out of range of any of the cameras at the station. Yet again, the elusive criminal had left nothing behind to tie to his identity.

Now, a sitcom rerun she'd seen several times played out with muffled voices in the corner, but she couldn't concentrate on the storyline. Instead, she kept her unseeing stare transfixed on the dancing flames in the fireplace. The orange sparks flicking in the stone hearth were mesmerizing, but their warmth didn't penetrate the constant chill in her bones.

"Why don't you sleep?" Cruz asked as he walked into the room, concern creasing the lines on his forehead.

She offered him a weak smile. "I've tried, but no matter how tired I am, I can't drift off. Have you learned anything more?"

A flash of hesitancy skittered across Cruz's face, and he crossed the room to sit on the other side of the large, gray sectional. "Bobby got a new door and better locks installed at your house. He texted that he left a new set of keys in my mailbox. There was some sort of emergency he had to tend to at the Miller's Farm, so he didn't want to stop and bring the keys up to the door. But that's fine by me. The man never stops talking."

She frowned. "That's not what I meant, and you know it."

He grabbed a blanket from off the back of the couch and tossed it her way. "Still trying to take all these damn lines and tie them together. Nothing concrete has come from anything we've found."

"Have you called any of the women yet?" The soft blanket covered her feet, and she slid it up to her chin, burrowing into its warmth. The last twenty-four hours had been so full of chaos, Cruz hadn't gotten much of a chance to connect with anyone who could help put all the pieces of this horrible puzzle together. Hopefully the women who'd also been targeted could help shed some light onto why this was happening.

"Not yet." Cruz let his head loll back and squeezed the bridge of his nose. "I'll let you know when we do. I feel like we're at a dead end when we should be full steam ahead. This guy's been busy the past twenty-four hours, yet we keep coming up empty at every crime scene he leaves behind."

She shuddered and wrapped the blanket tighter around herself. "He knows what he's doing."

"Exactly. I can guarantee you aren't his first victim. He's

had practice and knows how to cover his tracks. Knows how to fly under everyone's radar."

His description of the man who'd broken her life to pieces like a wrecking ball transported her back to the memories of a time she tried so hard to forget. Back to another man who had once stormed into her life and left her feeling like she was drowning, unsure of which way was up. A man who, although was always right in front of her face, knew how to hide who he really was—what he really wanted.

Cruz inched toward her. "Are you all right?"

Squeezing her eyes shut, she scrubbed her fingertips down her face, wishing she could peel away every awful image in her mind. When she opened her eyes, she stared into Cruz's soft, blue irises. Empathy poured from him, and for the first time, she yearned to spill all her secrets. To tell this man in front of her, this man who'd been her closest friend and who possessed the sweetest soul, all the horrors that plagued her past.

The words sat trapped in the back of her throat. Saying them out loud wouldn't lessen the pain, and a familiar fear kept her mouth closed. Her misery locked inside.

Erasing the space between them, Cruz tucked his thumb under her chin. "I'll stop him. I'll find a way."

His declaration loosened fear's hold on her confession. Cruz had done everything he could, including giving her a place to stay. She couldn't let him think she lacked confidence in him or his ability to do his job. Moistening her dry lips with her tongue, she grabbed hold of the tiny voice inside her, screaming to just let it all out—all the hurt and shame. "This isn't the first time I've been in a situation like this."

Cruz's body went rigid. He opened his mouth then

snapped it closed. His gaze stayed glued on hers, his eyes narrowed and taking in every single detail.

The wheels spinning in his head were clear as day, and she could see him battling between asking questions and wanting to give her the space she needed to open up. If her heart wasn't beating with the speed of a hummingbird's wings, she'd almost laugh at her ability to read him so well.

"Before I go any further, I'll tell you right now, there's no way it's the same person."

Cruz tilted his head to the side, doubt creating ripples on his normally smooth forehead. "How can you be sure?"

Unflinching, she held his stare. "Because the man who raped me before is dead."

There it was, the statement she'd never made now tossed into the lap of this charming room like a bomb. The word scratched at her throat like stones, making her crave a cold glass of water. She'd never spoken it aloud to anyone. Not her Ma when she returned home from the service. Not Brooke when they struck up the purest friendship she'd ever known.

Leaning forward, Cruz dropped his hand to her knee and gave a gentle squeeze through the blanket. "I'm so sorry. I...I don't really know what to say."

A sad smile lifted her lips. She relaxed her hand over his, giving into the warmth and comfort his simple touch brought her. She'd vowed she'd never rely on anyone for those feelings of peace again—not after falling victim to a man who used those needs against her—but right now, in this moment, Cruz's presence and simple gesture was like a soothing balm over her battered soul. "There's nothing you can say. Nothing can erase what happened or make it better. But I wanted you to understand those moments when I snap or get overwhelmed, my reaction isn't because of you."

"Zoe, you don't need to tell me anything you don't want. Especially if only to make me not question why you're upset with all this." He shoved a hand through his hair, tousling it in the process. "Hell, *I'm* upset. I'm pissed. And knowing you've gone through this before—but worse..."

She sucked in a large breath, the motion expanding against the tightening in her chest. "What happened last night was terrifying, but what happened the last time..." Held-in tears stung her throat. A part of her wanted to pull the blanket over her head and hide. Pretend like she could disappear. Forget everything that happened. But that was a silly fantasy. She needed to face her problems head on, no matter how painful. "I knew him—trusted him even—and when the unthinkable happened, there was no one for me to turn to. He took so much away from me. So much that I'll never get back."

The tears fell then, unhindered over her cheeks, plopping onto her lap. A sob caught in her throat, and for the first time, she didn't choke it down. She let the loss and grief break away like an avalanche.

Cruz folded her into his arms and rubbed a palm over her back. "Shhh. It's okay. I've got you. You don't have to tell me anymore. Not if it's too hard."

She clung to him, letting herself wallow in all the emotions she'd repressed for so long. But a tiny bit of relief seeped through the agony, luring her into opening up all the way. By baring her soul to this man who meant so damn much to her, she'd finally unburdened herself. Finally spoken her truth.

Or at least most of it. She couldn't tell him everything. No, some secrets were meant to be kept. Especially ones that were the reason for keeping her heart tucked away forever. Even from a man like Cruz. Because the day would come when he'd want a wife and family. And she loved Cruz too much to allow him to settle for a woman who couldn't give him those things.

A woman who could never give him children.

CRUZ STRUGGLED NOT to tighten his hold on Zoe. It wasn't just his overwhelming need to soak up all her misery that had him keeping her pressed against his body, but the way her trust in him made his heart shudder. He wanted to prove he was worthy of that trust.

She pulled out of his arms and wiped her eyes. Her nose burned red and specks of black from her mascara scattered along her cheekbones. "I'm fine. I want to get this out. Once and for all."

He sandwiched her hand between his, resting them on his lap. "What do you mean once and for all? Didn't you tell the police what happened? Your family?" Lincoln could be a pain in his ass, but there was nothing he wouldn't confide in his brother. Not to mention their mother who always stood by their side. His father would have, too, if he hadn't been killed in the line of duty when Cruz and Lincoln were boys. No matter where he stood in his life, how low things had gotten, his family was always there.

Even when he'd pushed them away.

Zoe slipped her hand from his, and the loss of her touch sent an icy blast of longing through him. "I've never told a soul."

Silence stretched between them, nothing but the crackling fire interrupting the stillness. A million questions burned his throat, but he didn't want to bombard her. He'd give her the time she needed to open up. He grabbed a handful of the blanket covering Zoe to keep from reaching out to her again. She didn't need his touch—his comfort—she needed his patience.

"I met a guy when I was stationed in Afghanistan. We patrolled together. He was everything I always wanted." Her words wobbled, and she focused on the motion of her fingers pulling at a string from the blanket. "He was handsome and smart. Strong and brave. We both missed our homes and families, and he was always doing these little things to show me he cared."

Cruz scraped his thumbnail over his jean-clad thigh, already hating this guy.

"One night, we snuck away. Things started moving too fast for me, and I asked him to stop. He refused. Said I was a tease. He took what he wanted, walked away, and never spoke to me again." She glanced up and the devastation in her eyes sucked the air from his lungs.

"What an asshole. But didn't you have a commanding officer you could tell? A friend? Anyone to help you?"

She shook her head, and her messy hair swirled around her face.

Unable to resist, he cradled his palm around her jawline and swiped away a tear with the pad of his thumb. "You have me."

She smiled through her tears. "And you mean the world to me."

Her words constricted his throat, and the need to know what she tasted like—to feel her lips on his—almost had him leaning forward. But now wasn't the time. Not after she'd laid herself bare, exposing something she'd kept inside for way too long. "What happened to the bastard?"

"He was in a tank that rolled over an IED. No one survived. And when I heard the news, all I could feel was relief. Like some cosmic form of justice had taken place. Then guilt crashed down on me. How could I feel anything but sadness and loss for something so tragic? Especially one that took the lives of some good men."

He dipped his chin so she couldn't avoid meeting his eyes. "No one would blame you for how you felt."

She shrugged, as if not believing him.

Shifting to her side, he slid his hand from her face over her shoulders, tucking her close. "If he wasn't already dead, I'd make sure to kill him anyway." He might mean every word, but he lightened his tone with a soft chuckle.

Zoe gave an indelicate snort and rested her head on his shoulder.

Instinctively he wrapped her tight, securing her to him with a firm hand. He'd sit like this all night if it was what she needed, but a quick glance at the cable box below the all-but-muted television alerted him to the time. "Have you eaten anything today besides that pastry?" He'd insisted she take the turkey sandwich with them when they left the studio, but she'd thrown the entire thing in the trash after he'd found the threatening note on his windshield.

"Not really." A large yawn mumbled her words. "But that cry made me feel like I could actually get some sleep."

As much as he'd love to let her fall asleep right there, in his arms in front of a fire, he needed to make sure she took care of herself. Yes, sleep was important. But so was food. "How about you get ready for bed, and I'll make you something to eat."

Lifting her head, she fixed him with an annoyed stare. "You've tried to get me to eat all day. I'm not a child. I can feed myself if I'm hungry."

He couldn't help but laugh. "Nothing big, but I'm hungry

and was about fix myself something. We can share a light meal, then both get a good night's sleep."

She sighed then stretched her arms above her head. The blanket fell to the floor and a thin strip of exposed skin gleamed above the waistband of her black yoga pants. "Fine."

His fingers itched to caress the sensitive skin. Instead, he rubbed his palms over his thighs and watched her waltz down the hallway toward his guest room. The subtle sway of her hips made his stomach muscles clench.

He swallowed hard and jumped to his feet, needing some space. Some air. He'd run out and grab the keys from the mailbox. He'd wanted to do it earlier, but Zoe needed him more. Snaring all his attention, making him want to jump back in time and fix the shitstorm that had surrounded her when she'd been so vulnerable. That might not be possible, but he could stop what was happening now. He wouldn't let her down the way she'd been let down before.

The way he'd let down Diana.

With a slight tremor rocking his core, he crossed over the plush carpet to the narrow entryway at the front of his home. Not bothering to grab a jacket, he slipped on his sneakers and rushed out the door. The cold air slammed against him but did nothing to cool the flames that Zoe had ignited.

Damnit, how had she gone from his good friend to a woman who turned his blood to fire in one day? Sure, he'd always thought she was a knock-out, but this ache in his chest was something more. He couldn't put his finger on what opened his eyes to how much Zoe meant to him, but one thing was for sure, there was no turning back.

Jogging down the red-brick sidewalk to the concrete

driveway, he made his way to the mailbox by the road. Streetlights beamed against the darkening sky, not quite late enough for the stars to burn in the night. The street was quiet, most of his neighbors were home for the evening, and the subtle outline of the Smoky Mountains dominated the skyline. He opened the mailbox, retrieving the keys, and smiled at the pepper spray Bobby had attached to Zoe's new keyring. Gotta love a town that looked out for one another the best way they knew how.

Boom!

Cruz whipped toward the blast and spotted smoke billowing toward the sky a few doors down. Securing the keys in his hands, he ran back to the house and threw open the door. "Zoe! Stay inside! I'll be back!" He tossed the keys on the floor mat and took off toward the explosion.

9

Zoe escaped into the privacy of the guest room, shut the door, and took a steadying breath. She'd shed a hundred-pound burden in the last fifteen minutes —a burden Ty forced on her that night so long ago.

A burden that had grown tenfold after she'd discovered she was carrying his child, which resulted in an ectopic pregnancy that stole her ability to have children and almost took her life.

She pressed her hands to her stomach, a familiar ache built in her soul. Ty had taken so much more from her than he'd ever realized. He'd not only taken her innocence, he'd taken her chance at a future—a family.

Why hadn't her path connected with Cruz when she was younger? From the first time they'd met, four years before when they'd both sat at the bar eating dinner at the Chill N' Grill, she'd felt an instant connection. Not just attraction, because let's face it, she'd have to be blind not to be drawn in by his mega-watt smile and cobalt blue eyes. It was something more that had cracked through her shell. His kindness and warmth and ability to make her feel like she held all his attention all the time. He was a great friend, always there when she needed him—whether it be changing the oil in her car or taking her to see a movie he didn't really want to watch. She'd give anything to change her circumstances, to see if there could be more.

But that wasn't an option. She'd continue to value his friendship and do what she did best. Shove all her real feelings so far down, she could almost fool herself into believing the narrative she set.

Almost.

Blinking away tears, she found her bag stuffed in the closet and rummaged through for her pajamas. Damnit, she should have packed the cute matching set with the black button-up collared-shirt and pants. Instead, she burrowed into an old Army hoodie, secured her hair on the top of her head in a messy bun, and opted to keep on her yoga pants. She'd change into a pair of ratty shorts before she went to sleep.

Boom!

Straightening, Zoe strained her ears. Was that an explosion of some kind? It didn't sound close enough to be of danger to her or Cruz, but did someone need help? She ducked back into the hall, turning toward the kitchen. "Cruz?"

He wasn't there.

Had he heard the explosion and taken off outside? Or maybe gone into his bedroom to get something?

"Cruz?" she called again, louder this time.

Still no answer.

Hurrying around the butcher-block island that separated the kitchen from the living room, she quickened her pace to the little entryway. The front door was cracked, as if Cruz had rushed out and the door hadn't latched all the way in his haste to leave. The boots he'd kicked off when they'd returned to his house earlier weren't on the black mat under the coat rack, but something else was.

Crouching, she smiled at the keys Cruz must have tossed inside. Two keys, presumably for the new locks at her house, and what looked like pepper spray, were attached to the ring. She secured the pepper spray in her hand and stood, appreciation glowing inside her at Bobby's thoughtfulness.

Standing, she debated whether to look for Cruz outside. She strolled to the window. Maybe she could see where he'd gone, or at least where the blast had come from.

A hand clamped hard over her mouth. A scream ripped from her throat, but the leather glove muffled the sound. Terror flooded her system, but she couldn't give into it.

"You can't hide from me." The man hooked an arm across her waist and anchored her to him.

The harsh whisper grated against her cheek, and the faint scent of peppermint was like a punch in the gut.

She wouldn't let him win—let him scare her into submission. She wasn't some shrinking violet who didn't know how to defend herself. She needed to fight back. Show this asshole he'd messed with the wrong woman. She moved the tiny canister attached to her keyring around in her palm, searching for the trigger.

He tugged her backward, and she dug her heels into the floor. He tightened his hold, his forearm like steel against her stomach. "I'm not playing with you. Do you want me to cut you again? Because if you keep pushing me, I'll do a lot worse than I did last night."

She squirmed against her assailant's hold. Locating the little trigger at the top of the pepper spray, she raised her arm, aimed it behind her, and sprayed the mist. The pungent scent of harsh pepper and chemicals stung her nostrils, and she closed her eyes so the haze wouldn't blind her.

"Sonofabitch" He growled out the words, a gravely tenor became more pronounced in his voice.

He dropped his arms, and she shot forward.

Muttered curses sounded behind her, but she didn't stop. Her only thoughts were of getting out of the house and away from him.

She wrenched open the front door and hurled herself across the threshold. "Help me!" The cold wood of the front porch penetrated her thick socks, but she kept moving. Kept running. Not giving the sting of wind across her face a second thought as she catapulted herself down the three steps and into the front yard.

Red and blue flashes slashed across the darkening sky in the distance, the blare of sirens approaching. But no one was coming to save her. The police would charge right past, unaware of the monster closing in on her. She waved her arms above her head, her grip still tight on the can of pepper spray.

A plume of smoke puffed upward a few houses down. *Cruz.* She had to get to him—had to alert him to her danger. "Help!" She screamed as loud as she could through her ragged breaths as she sprinted across the yard. "Someone! Please help!"

COLUMNS OF SMOKE poured from the blown-out siding of the stand-alone garage three doors from Cruz's house. No flames appeared to burn inside the destruction. Mr. and Mrs. Cogsly were in their eighties and seldom left their home. What in the world could have happened in their barely-used garage to cause such devastation?

Needing to make sure no one was injured, Cruz covered his mouth with the inside of his elbow and approached the building. No fire was evident from his position just outside, but the smoke inhalation could be just as dangerous. "Hello? Is anyone inside?"

No answer.

Squinting, he tried to peer through the dense fumes. Nothing but swirls of gray filled the room. The ashy scent of the soot mixed with a hint of metal and burned his nose. He wanted to charge in but putting himself in danger wouldn't do anyone any good.

He ran to the Cogsly's front door and pressed the bell three times in rapid succession. He was familiar enough with his neighbors to know they were hard of hearing and usually in bed before the sun even set.

Mr. Cogsly appeared with a troubled frown in a ratty, flannel robe. His white hair stood on end, and he dotted a handkerchief to his bulbous nose. "Cruz? Is that you? What on earth is going on?"

"Is Mrs. Cogsly inside with you?"

"Why, yes. Of course. We were in bed when we heard some kind of explosion. I called the police. Is everything all right?" He leaned to the side as if searching for the source of the disruption, but the ruined garage wasn't visible from where he stood.

Sirens blasted through the whisper of the wind and soft crackling of moving branches.

Cruz glanced over his shoulder. Dispatch had sent help quickly. "Looks like something exploded in your garage, sir. I tried to get a look, but the smoke is too dense. I wanted to make sure you and your wife were okay, but I'll let the firefighters take care of what's inside." He could handle the problem if needed, and properly outfitted, but no reason to rush into a potentially dangerous situation.

Mr. Cogsly's sleepy eyes widened. "Oh no. What in heaven's name could have blown up out there?"

"Hard to say, but as soon as there are answers, I'll make sure someone lets you know. Better for you and you wife to wait inside. I'm sure one of the responding officers will want to speak with you."

"Oh, okay. I can do that."

Cruz dipped his chin before turning to watch the approaching parade of emergency vehicles proceed down the street.

"Help!" a woman's voice yelled.

Cruz's pulse picked up, and he ran toward the smoldering garage. Had he missed something? Was someone actually in there?

"Someone! Please help!"

His heart kickstarted, beating with an unforgiving force. "Zoe?" He called out her name as he sprinted toward his house. He'd left her alone. Unprotected.

He wedged through a line of towering bushes that acted like a fence between the Cogsly's and their next-door neighbor. Dry twigs scraped against his skin and scratched his jaw. He burst out the other side and spotted Zoe running toward him, her hair flying with the wind behind her, eyes wide and filled with fear.

"He was in the house." Her pitch spiraled higher with each frantic word. "He grabbed me."

Dread curled around his stomach like a clenched fist. He pushed his pace faster until he reached her, and she fell into his open arms. "I got you. You're okay."

Her body trembled against him, her composure slipping

with each ragged breath. "In the house. Held me. Sprayed him with pepper spray."

Her statement was jumbled and hard to understand, but that didn't matter now. If her attacker had been inside his home, Cruz needed to figure out where he was now. He rubbed a palm over the back of her head as he surveyed the surrounding area. No shadows lingered nearby. No figures lurked anywhere he could see. "Did he follow you? Is he outside?"

"I think he came after me. I don't know. I was too scared to stop and look. I had to run. Had to find you."

"I shouldn't have left you. I'm so sorry." Guilt crushed his lungs. He'd vowed to protect her, and he'd left her inside his home, ran away without a second thought. Instinct had taken over, another fire needed put out, and all the training that kept him alive on the force kicked in and he'd ran.

And the gut reaction that was such a big part of him was the reason Zoe was put in danger. Just like with Diana. Realization struck him like a roundhouse kick to the head. He was a cop, through and through, and the decisions he made would always put the people he loved at risk.

He squeezed Zoe tighter. He wanted to comfort her, but the truth was making him see everything so much clearer. It didn't matter if his eyes—and heart—were open to Zoe. He could never be with her. Never trust himself to love her.

He'd already gotten one woman he loved killed, no way in hell he'd let it happen with another.

10

Not even the sweet smell of one of Chet's freshly baked cinnamon rolls could coax anything but irritation and just plain pissyness from Zoe the next morning. After returning to Cruz's home the night before, a weird tension had hung thick in the air between them. The intruder was nowhere to be found, and she'd spent another sleepless night tossing and turning.

At the retreat, she'd skated through the morning yoga class, which she, with reluctance, held inside again. After, she'd made a quick beeline for the kitchen. Zoe could tell everyone she'd hurried away in order to lend a much-needed hand, but she'd craved an escape from the constant eyes of the strangers in her class.

Especially Dusty, who'd showed up again with a warm smile and stiff, uncoordinated moves. Moves that were as cringe-worthy as they were endearing. Or at least would have been had she found herself in a different situation where she didn't gaze upon every man she encountered as her possible attacker.

Or if the redness in his eyes hadn't set her on high alert.

Chet opened the oven and a blast of heat brought out the drool-inducing scent of cinnamon with a hint of vanilla. The retreat's mountain-man of a chef had a white apron looped about his neck and tied around his thick, muscular frame. His familiar flannel, red today, covered his muscled arms. His long, chestnut beard hugged his handsome face, but did nothing to detract from the constant sadness in his brown eyes. A sadness that hadn't left since his cousin was murdered the summer before.

He placed the hot tray of buns on top of the stove then tossed an oven mitt on the counter. "You don't have to be here, ya know? I can handle this."

Gone was the hint of annoyance that usually accompanied this statement, which only increased her own irritation. She didn't want anyone feeling sorry for her or expect her to just sit by, scared and alone. She wouldn't just watch her life pass while she waited for some jerk to be caught. Not going to happen. She whipped the whisk through the icing she'd prepared, the bright red bowl bouncing in her firm grip. "I'm fine."

"I'm sure ya are but try telling that to the icing you're beating to a pulp."

"I'm not beating anything. I'm mixing." Rolling her eyes to the ceiling, she slowed the pace of her whisk. The same mahogany-colored wood that dominated the lobby of the retreat covered the ceiling in the kitchen, but the beams here ran the length of the room with a few positioned the opposite direction to make it appear as though square indents were built into the ceiling.

She stood at the massive island in the center of the room and concentrated on the gentle flick of her wrist as she continued stirring. When she'd been upset about a bully at school or missing her parents, her grandma used to usher

her into the kitchen. They'd bake and talk for hours until something delicious filled their bellies and Zoe's problems were fixed. Being here with Chet, helping to get breakfast on the table, was the best place for her to be right now.

"Whatever you got to tell yourself. Just don't mess up my icing." Pivoting, he set the cooling tray beside her.

She cocked a hip and pointed the wire whisk at him. Drips of icing splattered on the tile floor. "Your icing? You mean the icing I just labored over and carefully folded together?"

Chet stuck a spoon in the bowl. The topping coated the tip of the spoon, and he stuffed the utensil in his mouth. "Not bad. But stop whipping the shit out of it." He offered a rare smile and crossed the room to the industrial-sized refrigerator, pulling out sliced fruit that had been prepared the night before.

"It's okay to not be fine," Chet said. "I wasn't when Julia died. Hell, I'm still not. But I show up every day because people depend on me, and because the kitchen is my therapy. Keeps me calm. I get why you're here, and although I don't say it much, it's appreciated."

The string of words may have been the longest she'd ever heard from the quiet man, and they warmed her heart. Chet didn't open up much, but he'd given her the exact wisdom she needed. "Thanks," she said, smothering the sticky buns with icing. The thin topping melted on impact, soaking into the sweet bread and running over the sides.

Brooke poked her head around the corner of the doorway and interrupted the moment with a concerned frown. Her always present pink lipstick coated her lips, and she'd pulled her hair away from her face in a low ponytail. "Morning. Ready for me to start taking the food out to the dining room?"

Zoe spread the last bit of icing and tossed the dirty pastry brush in the bowl. "Cinnamon buns are ready."

"They smell amazing, like always." Brooke crossed the room in a hurry and gave Zoe a quick squeeze. "You okay?"

"She's fine," Chet said, arranging a selection of breads and bagels for toasting. "Let's move before the food gets cold."

She shot Chet an appreciative look. Brooke would hound her with questions soon enough, but Zoe didn't want to deal with it now. She busied herself by shuffling sweet and savory breakfast foods from the kitchen to the dining room next door. White linen cloths covered the square tables. A smaller version of the stone hearth from the lobby housed an intimate fire, and the floor-to-ceiling windows showed off the picturesque lake at the back of the lodge.

Zoe stared at the serene scene she never tired of. Evergreen trees dominated the landscape, keeping the vibrant green intact and bountiful even in the harsh January weather, and blocking the view of most of the guest cabins nestled along the path. A thin film of ice covered the lake, banishing the lapping waves beneath it.

Brooke nudged against her shoulder. "Everything's pretty much done. I told Chet I'd clean the kitchen later. Let's get out of here for a little bit."

Hesitation twisted Zoe's lips, and she tore her gaze from the window to study her friend. Brooke's petite stature meant the top of her head barely reached Zoe's chin. But Brooke had enough gusto and stubbornness to get what she wanted, when she wanted it. She was a firecracker with an amazing heart, but Zoe wasn't ready to open up and spill her feelings. Not after laying her soul bare last night. It was too much too soon, even with her best friend. "I don't really want to talk right now."

"Who said anything about talking?" Brooke hooked up an eyebrow and smirked.

Curious, Zoe followed Brooke out of the dining room, leaving behind the subtle din of the handful of guests who'd decided to trudge through the cold to get breakfast. "Where are we going?"

Brooke cast a glance over her shoulder as she hurried down the wide hallway that connected the dining room and kitchen to the lobby. "Good. You're already wearing your tennis shoes."

Zoe jogged to catch up with her friend. "How do your short legs carry you so quickly?" Usually, Brooke was the one struggling to keep pace with Zoe, but this morning she moved as if a fire was lit beneath her.

"Places to go and all that." Brooke waved at a middle-aged woman sitting in a cozy, oversized chair by the lobby fire, book in hand. "Good morning, Mrs. Parson! Hope to see you later for that art class you talked me into."

Mrs. Parson laughed. "I wouldn't miss it," she said, then returned her focus to the book she'd been reading.

"Art class?" Zoe asked. Brooke was great with a hammer and nails but held no artistic ability with a canvas and brush. "Are you taking Brittany's painting class?"

Brooke turned the corner beside the check-in desk and headed toward the gym. A grunt tumbled from her mouth. "Mrs. Parson arrived a few days ago. Very shy. Quiet. Her paperwork mentioned she was crafty and painted. I recommended Brit's class, but she wouldn't commit. Heck, the woman didn't leave her room for two days. So, I said I needed extra attention Brit couldn't offer in class, but maybe Mrs. Parson could. Today's class number two."

Arriving in front of the double glass doors, Brooke swept them open and waited for Zoe to step through. "I hated yoga when I started that," she continued. "But I went because of you, then to help my shoulder after I was shot, and now it's actually tolerable."

A deep chuckle escaped Zoe's chest. As a former police officer, Brooke was athletic, but her body wasn't naturally limber. Yoga was a struggle for her but had helped her recovery move along at a quicker pace. Now Brooke attended a couple of Zoe's classes a week, grumbling the entire time. "You love it, and you know it. Now why are we here?" She cast a hand in front of her, indicating the state-of-the-art gym she hardly ever stepped foot in.

Not that the gym Brooke had assembled for the guests at Crossroads Mountain Retreat wasn't everything a gym rat could dream of. One wall was made entirely of glass to capitalize on the mountain view, while the others were dominated by sparkly mirrors. Equipment of every shape and size littered the large space. There were even secluded rooms in the back where Zoe sometimes taught yoga classes.

But she much preferred the open-air classes outside or holding the class on the wide third floor landing. More space. Better views. Less Distractions.

With a wide grin in place, Brooke crossed over the black rubber on the floor, casting waves at a duo of men running on treadmills and greeting a woman lifting free weights in front of a mirror. "Yoga is great for finding your inner zen and all that, but I think you'd benefit from something else right now. I won't say I know how you feel, because I don't, but I *will* say I've been in a scary ass situation where I felt out of control. Where I didn't know what would happen, and no matter how smart or diligent I was, I was caught in the crosshairs of something I didn't understand."

Anxiety tightened Zoe's chest. When Brooke's life had been in danger, Zoe had never been more frightened.

Well, almost never, but the idea her best friend could be ripped away by her lunatic ex-boyfriend was terrifying.

Brooke stopped in front of a large, black punching bag and hooked an arm around it. The bag—almost as big as Brooke—hung from a thick chain bolted to an exposed beam along the ceiling. "When I get scared or angry or tired of talking about what was going on, I come here. Yoga and peace are great, but nothing tops beating the crap out of something to get out some frustration."

Crinkling her nose, Zoe studied the punching bag, then Brooke's face. The determined set of her jaw and fire in her brown eyes told Zoe that Brooke wouldn't back down. Zoe huffed out a dramatic sigh but smiled. "Fine. I can throw a punch as well as you."

Laughing, Brooke tossed her a pair of boxing gloves. "I have no doubt. I'll hold the back of the bag, so just try not to land one of those punches on my face."

"I'll do my best," she said, while fitting the cumbersome gloves on her hands.

The rough material confined the movement of her fingers, but she didn't want Brooke to realize how uncomfortable she was. Brooke was trying to help, and it wasn't like Zoe wasn't experienced in different forms of physical exercise. Army life had her running the gauntlet, but after leaving the service and everything she'd experienced there behind, she sought a more peaceful way of working her body and her mind.

Bouncing from foot to foot, she tested the weight of the gloves before she threw a fist forward and connected with the bag. The force of the hit vibrated her arm and shot to her shoulder. She shook out her shoulder and landed a punch with her other fist.

"Come on, Zoe. You can do better than that. Really let go. Don't think. Just react." Brooke barked out the order like a commanding officer, giving the bag a little shake with each shouted word.

Zoe gritted her teeth and shot her fist forward as hard as she could. She grunted and threw another punch and another and another. The grunt morphed into a scream of rage, tearing through her. All the feelings she'd battled the last two days—terror and anger and frustration—coursed through her with the beads of sweat dripping from her hairline. She'd already been through her nightmare, weathered the hurricane that tore into her life. Having to deal with the same freaking horror again wasn't fair. It wasn't right. She'd already proven herself a survivor. She shouldn't be expected to do it all over again.

"Zoe. You're okay. You got this."

Brooke's encouragement penetrated the haze of emotions threatening to suffocate her. She gasped for breath, the punches still flying, until she collapsed against the punching bag, holding it close to her body as sobs caught in her throat.

"Zoe?" Concern softened Brooke's voice.

The sob came loose, and the desire to rid herself of the stupid shame and guilt she'd carried with her for so long welled up in her faster than the tears in her eyes. She hadn't asked for any of this. For Ty. For the loss of a baby—the loss of the ability to bring life into this world. Hadn't asked for another man to storm into her life like a tornado and throw her around and around, leaving her scared and desperate for solid ground.

She had to let it out—let it go. Telling Cruz her story last night had loosened a huge part of that burden, but not all of it. Now was the time. She needed to purge, to rid herself of the toxic thoughts and memories if she ever wanted to move forward.

Straightening, she struggled to catch her breath and turned her head to wipe the tears from her face on her shoulder.

Worry pinched Brooke's face, and she let go of the bag. It dangled, the chain squeaking as it danced back and forth. "Are you okay?"

Panting, Zoe nodded. "I will be, but first we need to talk. There's something I'm finally ready to tell you."

11

C ruz couldn't help himself from casting glances all around as he and Lincoln motored along the dirt path that circled the lake at the retreat. Nothing but trees and an occasional bird overhead came into view. A view that would be breathtaking—a touch of frost glistening on the pine needles and the thin sheet of ice stretched over the expansive lake—if his mind wasn't a million miles away.

On a woman who'd tortured his sleep for a second night in a row, leaving him grouchy and exhausted. Not even the pot of coffee he consumed could penetrate the haze cloaked around him like a wool sweater—uncomfortable and unwanted.

Lincoln gave him a sidewise glance that told Cruz exactly what he was thinking—told him his brother knew what, or who, Cruz was looking for.

"Zoe won't be out here. No reason for her to be back by the guest cabins, and Brooke plans to keep her busy." Lincoln urged the golf cart faster, the fierce wind barreling through the open sides.

"I don't know what you're talking about." Cruz crossed

his arms over his chest, tucking his bare hands between his thick coat and body to keep them warm.

Lincoln snorted out a laugh as he turned the corner toward cabin number twelve. "I'm talking about you moving your head all over the damn place like you're looking for a lost dog or something. Because you've looked like shit the past two days, dude. I can only assume it's from the very pretty house guest staying across the hall from your bedroom."

"Could have something to do with a case I can't crack. You know, the one where there's a stalker loose in our town, tormenting women."

Lincoln cast him another quick look, lip hitched behind his scruffy facial hair. "Nah. It's Zoe. I don't know what your problem is. She's awesome."

"No, shit, but that's not the issue."

"Then what is?"

He fisted his hands as the plethora of emotions he'd battled the night before rushed back. He'd tell Lincoln all of it when the time was right. But that time wasn't now, as they drove toward Dusty Somerfield's cabin to question him. The man might be a guest at the retreat and took Zoe's class because he'd been dying to try yoga, but his interest in her didn't sit well with Cruz. "Later, man. I need to keep my head on straight right now and discussing anything personal will just get in the way."

"I get it. So tell me again. What'd you find out about Dusty that sparked your interest so much we had to schedule another interview right away?"

Man, Lincoln was good. A hint of a smile cracked through Cruz's shitty veneer he'd worn all day. His brother knew something was up, and he knew the best way to get

Cruz's mind off the personal and back on work. Even if the two problems overlapped.

Cruz had already told Lincoln what he'd found, making sure to leave out any details Zoe would want him to keep between them, but he'd go over it all again. "Dusty Somerfield was given a medical discharge from the army. No marks on his record. However, I did find he served in Afghanistan at the same time as Zoe."

"So did hundreds of other men," Lincoln said.

"True, but still something to explore." He didn't want to divulge too much about what had happened to Zoe while serving overseas, so he kept the rest of his opinions to himself. "I made some calls. Inconsistencies appeared that raised some red flags."

"Red flags we'll get to the bottom of right now." Lincoln motored the golf cart onto the narrow strip of gravel beside the cabin and cut the engine. "Hurry up, it's freaking cold."

"You're such a wimp," Cruz said with a chuckle. He jumped out of the cart and headed for the cabin.

From the moment Brooke had moved to town three years prior and transformed the abandoned camp into a retreat, he'd fallen in love with her plan. He'd grabbed a hammer and been by her side whenever he could, fixing up the cabins along the lakeshore. What once housed area children during the summer months were now cozy cabins fit for one.

Or two, in Brooke and Lincoln's case.

Bounding up the porch steps, he ran a hand along the smooth railing that boxed in the rectangular area. A rocking chair sat to the side of the door, a little stand beside it, facing the lake and mountains. Cruz had a great view at his place, but nothing like this. One day, he hoped to find a cabin tucked in the woods. Even if he had to live in it alone.

"You okay, man?" Lincoln stepped up beside him and frowned.

"Yeah. Just thinking." To avoid any further questions, he knocked on the door and waited.

A few beats later, the door swung open to a medium-sized man with his light hair cut military style. His sharp green eyes behind thick black frames were strained with a tinge of red. "Afternoon, Officers. Come on in."

When Cruz had reached out to Dusty, he'd been more than willing to meet with them and quickly set up a time for him and Lincoln to come out to the retreat. Cruz hadn't wanted to bring the man into the station, not without cause, and was grateful he was so cooperative.

But that didn't mean he wasn't hiding something. Maybe he was just smart enough to understand how to play the game. As a fellow officer, he'd be privy to how these investigations worked. The idea another policeman could be behind such violent crimes turned Cruz's stomach, but he couldn't ignore Dusty's multiple connections to Zoe.

Stepping inside, Cruz swept off his cowboy hat and waited for Lincoln to enter the room and Dusty to close the door before speaking. "Appreciate you agreeing to talk to us. Especially after speaking to my brother yesterday."

"Of course. Anything I can do. Please, have a seat. I'd offer you some food or drinks, but there's not much here." Dusty gestured toward the couch and recliner positioned around the fireplace in the main area.

The space, like the rest of the cabins, was one big room —except the bathroom which was located in the back. The studio-style cabin boasted a small kitchen and a double bed shoved in the far corner, a dresser pressed against the wall.

Cruz liked the openness. Nowhere for anyone to hide.

Opting to stay on his feet, he studied Dusty's earnest

face. He noted the tinge of red in his eyes. "You feeling all right?"

A line sliced through the center of Dusty's forehead, and he folded his arms over his chest. "Excuse me?"

Strong arms. Broad chest. Wouldn't have any trouble pinning down a woman or keeping her still.

"Your eyes are red. Allergies aren't really an issue this time of year." Cruz scratched his jaw, trying hard to keep a blank expression. He didn't want to tip his hand, but it was a hell of a coincidence Zoe blasted her attacker with mace the night before and Dusty's eyes were swollen and discolored this afternoon.

Chuckling, Dusty ran the pad of his index finger over one closed eyelid. "No random winter allergies here. Just a case of me being stupid and falling asleep with my contacts in last night."

"I hate when I do that," Lincoln said.

Cruz fought not to roll his eyes. He and Lincoln both had 20/20 vision.

"But anyway, what can I do for you guys? Officer Sawyer asked me a few questions yesterday about when I'd gotten into town and if I'd ever been to Pine Valley before. What more can I tell you?" Leaving Cruz and Lincoln standing by the door, Dusty strode over to the couch and sat on the armrest.

"Call me Lincoln. Officer Sawyer gets a little confusing."

"I can only imagine," Dusty said.

Irritation tightened Cruz's skin. He wasn't in the mood for chit chat. "Anyway, Lincoln remarked that you moved to Hampton County a year and a half ago." Red flag number one had been Dusty's proximity to all the unsolved rape cases in theirs and the county right next to them. Hampton County was located on the edge of both areas of land, the three counties connecting at the far east corner.

Dusty nodded. "That's right. After leaving the army, I wanted a fresh start. Somewhere completely new. I always loved vacationing in Tennessee as a kid, so I figured what the hell?"

"And you said you're from Ohio, right?" Lincoln strolled over to the recliner in the corner and sat, leaning back and hooking an ankle over his knee.

"That's right."

Getting antsy for answers, Cruz got straight to the point. "I noticed you had quite a lapse of time between your medical discharge and finding your job as a sheriff's deputy down here. A little digging uncovered you were turned down for two different positions closer to your hometown."

Frowning, Dusty straightened to his full height. He was broad but didn't stand taller than Cruz and Lincoln. If Dusty held Zoe against his chest, the top of her head would reach the other man's eye line. He'd have to comb through his notes and see how tall Zoe thought her attacker was.

Annoyance pinched Dusty's face. "And why were you digging at all? I answered all the questions yesterday. No need to go behind my back."

Cruz frowned, his mind spinning on the best approach to take. He didn't want to piss this guy off so he wouldn't cooperate, but also needed to show Dusty that he knew there was more to his story.

Wanting to put Dusty a little more at ease, Cruz circled round the back of the couch and pulled out a chair from the two-person table. He angled it so he faced both Dusty and Lincoln. "I don't want to be intrusive, but you know how it is when there's a crime to be solved. Every lead needs followed."

Dusty cocked his head to the side. "And I'm a lead to some crime in this town I've never been in?" He threw his hands in the air. "Hell, I haven't stepped foot in town. I've been stuck at this place in an attempt to aid my recovery. Though I don't see how yoga and cold-ass runs through the woods will help."

The last sentence was mumbled under his breath, though still clear enough to Cruz's ears. He'd come back to the bit about the yoga, but first he needed to know more about why Dusty's hometown wouldn't hire him to be on their local police force. "You're not a lead, more like someone I needed a little more information on. And while gaining that information, I was told there was an issue with you and one of the female officers on your hometown police force that kept you from getting a job. Is that correct?"

Dusty muttered something then paced across the mahogany floors. "Are you freaking kidding me right now? That shit's followed me all the way down to Tennessee?" He halted, red flushing his chiseled cheeks, and faced Cruz. "I swear to you, nothing happened. At least not what she said."

Lincoln dropped his foot to the ground and leaned forward. "What does that mean?"

Dusty blew out a long breath. "We flirted a bit one night. Things got a little heated. I owned up to that part. What I didn't know is the woman was married. When her husband showed up unexpectedly, she shoved me away and said I forced myself on her. I swear I'd never do something like that."

Cruz worked his tongue over his teeth, reigning in his thinning temper. What Dusty described was a lot like what had happened to Zoe. Only she hadn't been given a chance for anyone to believe her because no one had been in her corner.

"Tell me, have you ever met Zoe Peyton before your stay here?"

Dusty blinked, taking in the question. "The yoga instructor?"

Cruz nodded.

"No, never. Why would you think I have?"

"What about when you were stationed in Afghanistan?" Cruz pressed, studying the rigid set of Dusty's shoulders as he asked each question. Even if he was the man they were looking for, he wouldn't come out and tell him. The tells would be in the way he reacted to the questions. Zoe didn't mention remembering Dusty from overseas, but that didn't mean the man didn't remember her.

A dark scowl turned Dusty's face almost menacing. "Are you crazy?"

Lincoln rose to his feet.

"Just answer the question," Cruz said.

"No, I didn't know Zoe while I served in Afghanistan." Dusty narrowed his gaze, a spark lightening the green of his eyes. "Is she in some kind of trouble?"

Lincoln made his way back to the door. "We can't discuss that with you."

"Unbelievable," Dusty said with a derisive snort. "You show up for the second time, throw my past in my face, ask ridiculous questions, and won't even tell me why? Despite what you might have heard from your source in Ohio, I'm a damn good cop. If something's going on with Zoe, I can help."

Cruz joined his brother at the door. "You've told us everything we need to know. If I have more questions, I'll be back."

He ignored Dusty's grumbling and stepped into the cold afternoon. The sun might be bright, but its rays were deceptive, promising a hint of warmth that wasn't there. He waited until he was seated beside Lincoln in the golf cart before he spoke. "What do you think?"

"I think you know something you haven't told me that makes you suspicious of this guy. Either about him or Zoe, but my money's on Zoe." Lincoln reversed the cart onto the path. "If you want my help, you need to spill. All of it."

Cruz squirmed on the vinyl seat. Telling Lincoln about what happened to Zoe didn't sit right with him. "Zoe has to be okay with anything I tell you. I won't jeopardize her confidence."

"Then let's go talk to her. My guess is the girls are at Brooke's cabin right now." Lincoln tilted his head in the direction of a cabin in the distance—his and Brooke's cabin —and two figures rocking on the chairs on the porch.

Cruz's phone vibrated in his pocket, and he retrieved his device, swiping the screen to bring up a message. "Shit. Lou from the firehouse sent me information about the explosion last night. They found a homemade bomb."

Lincoln blew out a low whistle. "Those old neighbors of yours had a bomb in their garage?"

Cruz clenched his fist around the phone as anger beat a steady drum inside him. "He said the thing was activated from the outside. That bastard planned it all out. He watched and waited for his best chance, then set the bomb off when he knew I'd run off, leaving Zoe alone."

And Cruz had played right into his hand. Ran without making sure Zoe had any protection. He needed to be smarter, think his actions through more carefully, or Zoe would end up hurt because of him. Because he couldn't do his damn job.

Guilt smothered his chest. Maybe Zoe would be better off with someone else watching over her. If history had taught him anything, it was that he couldn't protect the woman he loved—not when he had a job to do. After he and Lincoln talked to Zoe, Cruz would give her a choice.

And if she was smart, she'd choose to stay far away from him.

12

The smooth surface of the lake glimmered like glass in the sunshine. Zoe wished she could skim her hand over the top, feel the icy layer that transformed the giant body of water into something out of a winter wonderworld. But knowing her luck lately, as soon as she placed any weight on the ice, she'd fall right through, caught in the darkest depths, never escaping.

The idea sent a chill through her. She pulled the red and black checkered blanket tighter around her shoulders and took another sip of wine. Daytime wine. A luxury one earned when spilling their guts for the second time in less than twenty-four hours.

Wyatt, Brooke's lovable brown and cream-colored mutt, padded over to her and rested his head in her lap. He cast his large brown eyes at her, begging to be pet. He'd barely left her side since they'd arrived and she'd told Brooke about what had happened with Ty. And this time, she left nothing out of her confession.

"Hey there, big guy." Zoe set her stemless wine glass on the little stand tucked beside the wooden rocking chair and ruffled the top of Wyatt's head. "Thanks for all the cuddles. I just love you so much."

"I'd say the feeling's mutual," Brooke said. She kept a steady rhythm in her own rocking chair, gaze fixed on Zoe instead of the whimsical lake scene in front of them. "How are you feeling?"

Zoe shrugged. "I don't know. Relieved to have someone who knows all that I've been through. Sad it's my story to tell. Scared about everything that's going on and pissed I'm in a shitty situation because of some damn man for the second time in my life."

"I'm glad you told me, and I'm sorry. For all of it. But, Zoe, just because you can't have your own children doesn't mean you can't have kids. There are options."

There it was. The statement she'd avoided hearing for so many years. One of the reasons she'd kept what happened a secret was because she didn't want to hear all the advice from people she loved. Brooke meant well, and she even had a valid point, but she would never understand what it felt like to have her choices ripped away in the blink of an eye. To lose not only her child, but her chance to bring another baby into the world at the exact same time.

It was soul crushing.

Focusing on the silky fur under her hands, she offered her friend a weak smile. "Right now, I'm emotionally spent. I can't discuss my options or my future or anything else."

"I understand, but if you change your mind, I'm here."

"I know." A small frown turned down Brooke's pouty lips. "Is that Cruz and Lincoln in a golf cart?"

Zoe turned her gaze toward the gravel path. The bright sun blinded her, and she shielded her eyes with her hand. "Looks like it. What are they doing here?" A hint of worry lifted the last syllables of her question. Had they come looking for her? What else could have happened now? Or maybe they'd found her attacker...

Brooke set her glass beside Zoe's on the little stand and rose, waving at the approaching men.

Lincoln turned the golf cart onto the narrow strip reserved for parking beside the cabin. Vehicles were too big to fit on the path around the lake, so the retreat provided golf carts for all the guests to get back to their temporary living quarters. Lincoln had claimed one when he'd moved in with Brooke, painting it the same shade of blue as the Tennessee Titan's jerseys. A decision that annoyed Brooke and amused Zoe.

Cutting the engine, both men hopped out of the cart. Wyatt lifted his head to watch them approach, then barked once before bounding forward. He jumped first on Lincoln, then Cruz, offering them both welcoming licks with his slobbery large tongue.

Cruz crouched low and slung an arm over the big dog, using his hand to ruffle his side.

Lincoln met Brooke with a quick kiss on the cheek. "Hi, beautiful."

Brooke preened, her smile wide.

Zoe tried to ignore the dizzying wave of jealousy that was released when she saw Brooke and Lincoln together. She was thrilled for the two of them. Brooke had been through hell and back and deserved every happiness life had to offer. And she couldn't have hand picked a better match for her friend. But seeing the two of them reminded her of everything she'd grown up wanting and didn't have— a family of her own to shower with all her love. Love that she hadn't been able to give to her own parents.

"What were you two doing on the other side of the lake?" Brooke settled back into her seat.

Cruz straightened and leaned against the porch railing.

Zoe studied him. Something was off. Just like it had been last night after the excitement died down and she and Cruz were left alone at his house for the night. The sweet, compassionate man who'd held her and listened to her story had been replaced with someone whose nerves could practically be seen bouncing on his skin. He'd avoided Zoe, claiming they needed rest, then locked himself away in his room, leaving so early this morning she hadn't even caught a glimpse of him. Dark circles hung low under his eyes, and the tight set of his jaw screamed his agitation. He kept his gaze on his boots, and a defeated droop in his shoulders relayed a sadness she seldom saw in him.

Lincoln strode over and took up the spot beside Cruz. His jaw, so much like Cruz's, was covered in a few days' worth of scruff, and although a seriousness shone in his blue eyes, no sadness haunted his energy.

"We needed to talk to Dusty Somerfield," Lincoln said, crossing his feet at the ankles as he rested the small of his back against the railing.

"I thought you spoke with him yesterday." Zoe moved forward on her seat. "Why did you speak with him again?"

Cruz finally met her gaze. "I found some disturbing information regarding him earlier today. I needed to ask him about it."

Zoe crossed her arms over her chest, acting as if this disturbing information didn't affect her. She refused to be brushed aside. "Such as?"

"A woman in his hometown accused him of forcing himself on her," Cruz said.

"What?" Brooke shrieked and shot back to her feet. "That wasn't in any of the paperwork he sent into the retreat. Guests here are thoroughly vetted. I take no chances of letting a criminal slip through. Law enforcement or not, I personally make sure none of the guests have any marks on their records."

Cruz held up a palm as if to calm Brooke down. "No charges were filed. Nothing was on his record."

Zoe's stomach churned. "Did he rape her?"

"He claims he didn't force himself. That he didn't know she was married. The husband caught them, so the woman panicked and lied."

Zoe squeezed her eyes closed for a beat before opening her lids again and fixing her stare on Cruz. "Do you believe him?"

"I don't know."

Her heart sank. She'd been attacked and hadn't reported it because she didn't think anyone would be on her side. Cruz's skepticism of another woman's claim was like a dagger to her heart. Tears misted her eyes, but she refused to break eye contact. "Did you believe *me*?"

THE HURT REFLECTED in Zoe's eyes squeezed Cruz's gut, and her question cut him at the knees. "Of course I believed you. How can you even ask me that?" He'd held her in his arms last night, wanting nothing more than to erase all of her pain. He'd meant what he'd told Zoe. If Ty was still alive, he'd hunt him down and make him pay for what he'd done.

Zoe swiped her eyes and grabbed a wine glass, bringing it to her lips and gulping down half the contents.

Lincoln cleared his throat, curious about the reason for the thick tension hanging in the air. "Zoe, I'm not sure what's going on, but I hope you trust me enough to fill me in. Cruz is tight-lipped and said he can't tell me your story, but if I'm assisting with this case, and it's something that can help, I might need to know. At least the bare bones."

Zoe sighed. "Can Brooke tell you? I can't go over it again. At least not right now."

Lincoln nodded. "Absolutely."

"There's more, Zoe," Cruz said. "The bomb from last night was planted by someone. It was a homemade device. Someone activated it to get me out of the house so they could get to you."

Zoe's mouth fell open, her fair skin now ashen. "Is no place safe? Nowhere I can go where this creep won't follow me?"

Wyatt trotted over to Zoe and rested his head in her lap.

Cruz swallowed his frustration. "I'm sorry. I should never have fallen for the ploy. I should have stayed with you."

Lincoln clicked his tongue. "You did what any other lawman would have done. You can't be blamed for some lunatic's actions."

Cruz bit down on his opinion. Although Lincoln was right, it was that exact reaction that would keep Zoe in danger. He chanced a glance at Zoe, who had her face pressed against Wyatt's head. She didn't disagree with Cruz but hadn't accepted his apology. Her lack of response constricted his chest, but he couldn't blame her for it. Hell, wasn't that what he wanted? Her to realize he wasn't the best option to keep her safe?

He cleared his throat, needing to get out the words he didn't want to say. "I don't think you should stay with me anymore."

Zoe's head shot up, eyes wide and confused. "What? Why not?"

"This guy knows you were at Cruz's," Lincoln said.

"Staying there would make as much sense as going back to your place. It isn't safe."

"What am I supposed to do? Run away and stay with some long lost relative? Bring danger to their doorstep, all while putting a hold on my life? I can't do that. I can't just press pause on my business." Her voice pitched higher and higher, each word puffing out on a stream of cold air.

Brooke placed a hand on Zoe's arm, forcing Zoe's panicked gaze her way. "You'll stay here."

Zoe blinked, as if taking in the suggestion. "I appreciate the offer, but I don't want to stay in one of the employee rooms. Those rooms should stay open for any staff members who need to crash for the night. They aren't meant for anything longer than that."

Brooke rolled her eyes. "Do you think I'd put you in a glorified dorm room by yourself?"

"But the cabins are all full," Zoe said. "And I wouldn't want to be tucked away by myself in the woods anyway."

"Not a cabin. The lodge. We have two rooms for guests who can't access the cabins back here." Brooke waved a hand to indicate the area around the lake. "One is open, and I don't have anyone scheduled to be in there for another two weeks."

Eyebrows raised, Zoe twisted her lips and locked eyes on Cruz. "Maybe."

He forced a tight smile. The idea of her being away from him physically pained him, but Brooke's suggestion made sense. Zoe would be safe at the lodge. Brooke and Lincoln would be nearby, not to mention the other staff who lived at the retreat. Plenty of people around to keep their eyes on things.

Zoe ran her fingers along the long bridge of Wyatt's nose. "I still don't want to be alone. Even here. Cruz, you just told me about Dusty's past. What if he's our guy? I don't want to be so close to him, knowing he could be watching and waiting."

Cruz scratched behind his ear. She had a good point. He couldn't strike Dusty Somerfield off his very short list of suspects. "If he's responsible, he'll know we're on to him after our conversation. He'll know we're watching him."

"Which could make him act more aggressively," Zoe said. "Which means I want you with me."

Her forceful tone had Cruz rearing back, but her words flooded him with warmth. "Zoe, I'm the reason this guy almost got to you last night. I can't keep you safe. If you don't feel safe in a room inside the lodge, maybe we can hire someone to protect you. Maybe assign a different officer just for your safety."

"Oh, shut up." Zoe waved away his argument like it was nothing more than an annoying gnat. "You did your job, and I got away. Got away and ran to *you*. I don't need someone I don't trust standing guard, treating me like a delicate flower. I'm capable of kicking some ass when required. What I need is my friend. Someone who can talk me through what's been found and respect me enough as a person to hear my input. To let me help catch this guy."

"She has a point." Shrugging, Brooke smirked.

Cruz ground his teeth together. What the hell was that look Brooke was making? Whatever it was, he didn't like it one damn bit.

Lincoln bumped Cruz's shoulder with his. "Agreed. This guy knows where you live. Has been in your house. Going back isn't the safest for you right now either."

"Oh, come on." Cruz threw up his hands. "I'm a police officer. I don't need to run and hide. Let him come back to my house and find me there alone. I'll show him what happens when he messes with me. Messing with someone I...care about." He altered his thundering train of thought before he said something so far across the line there'd be no turning back.

"Cruz, please," Zoe said. "If you care about me, stay with me here. I'll feel so much better if you do. If I remember correctly, there's two beds in the rooms in the lodge. We'll be just as comfortable here as we were at your place."

"Umm, actually, one bed." Brooke scrunched up her face but couldn't hide the tiny smile on her lips. "The other room inside that's occupied right now is the one with two double beds."

A light blush invaded Zoe's cheeks, but she stared at him with pleading eyes. Eyes he couldn't refuse.

"Fine." He sighed and ran a palm over his face. If the last two nights had been tough, what was to come would be borderline torture.

13

Zoe stepped inside the room she'd call home until her stalker was caught. As lovely as the space was —with the warm wood covering the walls and floors and thick beams zig zagging across the ceiling—she hoped she wouldn't be here long. Although, the idea of sharing the intimate room with Cruz made tingles of anticipation dance along her spine.

Well, it would if getting him to agree to stay with her hadn't been like pulling teeth.

Running her finger along the back of the brown leather couch, Zoe averted her gaze from Brooke so her friend couldn't read her thoughts. "The sofa looks comfortable. I can sleep here while Cruz takes the bed."

Brooke chuckled and pulled a spare pillow and blanket from the closet by the door. "Already thinking about sleeping arrangements, huh?"

Heat invaded Zoe's cheeks. "Shut up. I just want everything prepared for when Cruz gets back later. He was weird last night and today. I don't know why. Maybe telling him what happened between me and Ty was too much for him."

"Not a chance." Brooke tossed the extra bedding onto the old-fashioned steam-trunk-turned-coffee-table. "But he was acting strange earlier. I can ask Lincoln if something's up."

Opting for the tufted armchair in the corner, Zoe sat and studied the subtle differences in this room from Brooke's cabin. The counters were lower to the ground, allowing for easier access for anything on top of them. Brooke had laid out everything else in the same manner as the cabins. One large room. Fireplace in the corner, furniture centered around it. Queen sized bed shoved on the far wall and a kitchen area just large enough for the basic necessities.

In another situation, being stuck in this room with a handsome man would be almost romantic. But not like this. Not when a stalker was tracking her like prey, and she had no idea who was after her.

She returned her focus to Brooke's comment. "No, I'll ask him about it tonight." Or at least she would if she didn't lose her nerve. The last few days had been a whirlwind of emotions, with Cruz as her anchor. She would never have the future she really wanted with Cruz but didn't want to lose his friendship. He was too important to her.

On a sigh, Brooke plopped onto the middle of the couch. "I'm sure he's just preoccupied with everything going on. You know, with trying to find who's after you while figuring out his feelings."

Zoe frowned. "What do you mean?"

"Don't act like you don't know how he feels about you. It's so obvious. Has been for years."

As much as the idea of Cruz having feelings for her made a swarm of butterflies dance in her stomach, it also saddened her beyond belief. "You've officially lost it. Just because you found your happily ever after doesn't mean it's in the cards for the rest of us. Besides, I told you. I'm damaged goods. Cruz deserves better." Zoe raked her fingernail over the thick skin of her thumb, concentrating on the stinging pain.

"Zoe." Brooke spoke her name with too much compassion. Too much pity.

"Nope. We're done talking about this." Biting the insides of her cheeks to keep threatening tears in check, Zoe glanced around, searching for something to keep her busy. There was nothing. She didn't even have any bags to unpack. Cruz said he'd grab her stuff she'd already packed for his place, along with his own, and bring the bags to the retreat when he was off shift.

Needing to expel some pent-up energy, she hopped to her feet. "I have to do something. Does Chet need help getting things ready for dinner?"

Brooke shook her head. "Already done. Same with breakfast prep."

"How's that possible?"

"I interviewed someone yesterday. Had her come in and help me around the kitchen so I could see how well she worked. Chet isn't happy about it, but it needed to be done." Brooke winced, a bit of guilt shining from her dark eyes.

Zoe puffed out a frustrated breath. She agreed with Brooke, kitchen staff was a must, but with her business shut down for the day and no more classes scheduled at the retreat until the morning, she had nothing to occupy her time. Now, she didn't even have the monotonous work in the kitchen. "He'll get used to it. Is he around?" If he was upset, maybe they could lift each other's spirits.

"Nah. He took off after I introduced him to Mia. He didn't make the best impression on her, but she wasn't scared off. So bonus points there. She's settling into one of the employee rooms. Just moved to town and doesn't have a place yet. I told her she could crash here until she finds something."

Zoe debated strolling down the hall and introducing herself, but the idea of pretending to be cheerful and friendly didn't sit well. Better to wait until she was in a better head space. "I'll introduce myself to her later. Right now, I need to clear my mind. I'm going to grab a yoga mat from the gym and find a good place to do some self-reflection. Maybe some light stretching."

"Want company? I don't have a lot on my plate today." Brooke rose, her concern as bright as the sunlight streaming through the window.

"No, thanks. I haven't had a minute to myself since this whole nightmare began. I'll be fine."

Brooke nodded and took a step toward the door then turned back around. "Just let me know if you decide to go out. I don't want to be a pest, but I'll worry if I don't know where you are."

Zoe smiled, thankful for such a great friend. "I promise."

She watched Brooke leave then gathered the key and her phone before heading to the gym. She kept her head down, not wanting to interact with anyone she passed along the way. Thankfully, at this point in the afternoon, most people were busy and not aimlessly wandering the wide halls. Picking up her pace, she sped across the lobby and rounded the corner to the gym. She'd grab a mat and head to the third floor. The area where she held class was too public for what she craved, but there were plenty of other rooms she could use that would give her privacy.

Opening the glass door, she stepped onto the black rubber floor. The sound of a treadmill chugged along, whoever ran on it panting as they kept pace. She headed to the studio-style room where she sometimes held class and scooped up a mat from the pile in the corner.

The hum of the treadmill stopped, the quiet buzzing of the florescent light the only sound bouncing off the high ceiling. Zoe tucked the mat under her arm and turned back to the door. Her heart lodged in her throat.

Dusty blocked the doorway, wiping a white towel across his sweaty face. "Hi, Zoe. How are you?"

Retreating a step, she swallowed her fear and forced a smile. Her mind spun, taking in her limited options for escape, or even anything to use as a weapon. She had a key in her waistband and a foam mat under her arm. If Dusty was stupid enough to come after her here, she had nothing but her personal skillset to use against him. "I'm good. You? Your eyes still look a little red."

Chuckling, he shook his head. "Still can't believe I slept in contacts. I know better." His full lips turned down, and he took a step forward. "I'm glad I caught you. Two officers spoke with me, and your name came up. I just want you to know, if there's anything I can do to help, just ask."

"I appreciate that, but everything's fine. Really, no big deal." The forced enthusiasm in her statement lifted her voice to a weird falsetto.

His bushy black eyebrows dipped down. "Are you sure? Really, I mean, I'm going a little crazy here just focusing on myself."

Her phone chirped in her side pocket. She grabbed it with an unsteady hand and checked the screen. *Cruz.* Just the sight of his name had relief flooding her system. "I'm sorry, but I have to take this. I'll talk to you later." Pressing accept, she lifted the phone to her ear and hurried past Dusty, making sure not to look back as she put this stranger who was way too interested in her as far behind her as possible.

CRUZ SAT at the bar inside the Chill N' Grill, gaze fixed on the clock mounted above the bar that gave the time as well as advertised his favorite beer. The Chill N' Grill was the best place to grab some food in Pine Valley and had always reminded Cruz a little bit of home. The rough-around-the-edges eatery didn't have the urban polish or constant flow of young talent searching for stardom like the honkey tonks in Nashville, but it was down-home country through and through.

Wade, the owner who often worked the bar, sauntered over with a toothpick between his thin lips and a dishrag slung over his shoulder. "Afternoon. Little late for lunch, isn't it?" He wiped off the already gleaming wood in front of Cruz and slid a coaster to his side.

Cruz grunted. The hours had ticked by as he and Lincoln uncovered more about Dusty Somerfield's past. Nothing else had popped up to cause concern, but the moment Cruz saw the man's blood-shot eyes the morning after Zoe had used pepper spray on her attacker, he'd gone to the top of his very *very* short list of suspects. "Worked through lunch. Zoe's meeting me, so I'll wait to order food in case she's hungry. I'll take a cola while I wait."

Wade scooped ice into a clear plastic cup then filled it with the dark liquid. "I heard about what happened. Too damn bad. Makes ya wonder what the hell's wrong with this world."

"Have you seen anyone who's given you a strange vibe? Any new customers lingering around?" Sliding the cup closer, Cruz slipped in a straw and took a sip. The cold soda cleared the dryness from his throat, the caffeine and sugar going straight to his head.

"Not that I recall." Wade scratched his index finger along the blond scruff of his naturally tanned jawline. "But I'll let you know if something pops up."

"Thanks."

"Looks like your little lady's here." Winking, Wade nodded toward the door.

A black, puffy coat all but swallowed Zoe's slim frame as she weaved through the scattered tables. She waved to a couple dining in the corner as she squinted, scanning the dimly lit room. When her eyes locked on him, he lifted a hand in greeting. A knot of tension loosened in his chest. Being away from her today had been harder than he'd expected, and he hadn't liked it.

Hadn't liked not being an arm's length away. Hadn't liked feeling as if a piece of him was missing.

Zoe smiled wide and settled onto the backless stool beside him. "Hi." She cast her grin toward Wade. "Hey there, stranger."

"Hey back, Darlin`. What can I get ya?" Wade's dimples deepened in his cheeks, and Cruz had to fight the urge to slap them off his face, taking the appreciative gleam in his eyes with them.

Tucking in her lips, she shrugged out of her coat and draped it over the empty stool to her right. "House salad with grilled chicken and water."

"All right, and you, Cruz?"

Stomach growling, Cruz decided on what he always got. "Burger and fries."

Wade nodded, filled a glass with water and placed it on a

coaster in front of Zoe, then disappeared behind a swinging door at the end of the bar.

"I'm glad you called," Zoe said, then took a sip from her glass. "Sitting at the retreat with nothing to do felt like a big waste of time."

"I wouldn't call staying safe a waste of time, but I get what you mean."

She rolled her eyes. "You mentioned wanting my help. What's up?"

"The woman who was raped at work finally got ahold of me. She's willing to talk. I asked if I could bring you along, and she agreed. Said she'd talk to anyone that would listen if it meant finally catching the guy who did this."

Excitement widened Zoe's eyes, and she jumped to her feet. "Well, let's go then. Wade can box all this up. We can eat later."

Cruz rested a hand on hers to guide her back down, and electricity shot up his arm, jolting his heart. He swallowed hard, forcing the desire a simple touch caused all the way down to the heels of his boots, then removed his hand. "No need to rush. Sit and eat, then we'll take off for Mill Hollow. The woman, Lexi, owns a bookshop in the center of town. She said she's there until seven tonight and will talk to us whenever we get there."

"But the sooner the better." Refusing to sit, Zoe hooked her arms over her chest and pinned him in place with a hard stare.

He laughed, forgetting how stubborn she could be. "No way I'm letting you in my cruiser with a damn salad. You'll make a mess. I'll shovel the burger in as fast as I can. Promise." He waved crossed fingers for good measure. Yes, he wanted to speak with Lexi soon, but he hadn't had a break all day. He needed just five minutes to fill his stomach and refuel.

Sighing, Zoe settled back on the stool. "Fine. What do I need to know about Lexi before we get there?"

"I only know the basics." Cruz cupped his palms around his cool glass. "She's twenty-nine and has owned her bookstore for two years. Lived in Mill Hollow her entire life, besides when she went away to college in Memphis."

Zoe tapped her finger against the bar. "Hard to see how I could have something in common with her. Mill Hollow might only be twenty minutes away, but I've never stepped foot there. And the name doesn't ring a bell."

Wade strode over with their plates and set them on the bar. "Need anything else?"

"Go ahead and get me the bill," Cruz said. "We'll take off as soon as we're done eating."

Wade dipped his chin then headed toward the register.

Cruz's mouth watered, and he picked up his burger and dug in. The taste of lean beef had him biting back a moan. He polished off half the burger before setting it down and dotting his mouth with a paper napkin. "You two are close in age."

"I've got a couple years on her." Zoe pointed a fork in his direction. Ranch dressing clung to the prongs.

Cruz chuckled and crunched on a fry. "You don't look a day older than twenty-five."

Shaking her head, she flashed him a smile.

"You're both business owners." He picked up his burger again and made quick work of finishing it off while Wade slid him the check.

Zoe's forkful of blackened chicken stopped halfway to her mouth. "True. But who runs from town to town, targeting bookstore owners and yoga teachers?" She dropped her fork in her salad and pushed the bowl away. "My appetite's gone again. Damnit, I just want this to be over."

"I know. Me too. You're right, though. The sooner we talk to Lexi, the better." He grabbed cash from his wallet and left it under his glass. "We'll take my cruiser."

He grabbed a handful of fries while Zoe shrugged into her jacket then led the way through the quiet bar. Placing his cowboy hat on his head, he grabbed his coat then held the door open for Zoe, following her into the frigid air. The sun had started its descent, hanging low with its beams burning a deep orange. Zoe beat him to the passenger side, so he hurried to the driver's door and climbed inside.

"Hurry and crank up that heat." Zoe rubbed her hands together.

He turned over the engine and blasted the heat, angling the vents toward Zoe. "Shouldn't take too long to get there. Lincoln also sent over information about a woman whose house was broken into. I think she's worth speaking to as well. We can stop to see her once we're done with Lexi."

Zoe clicked on her seatbelt. "Sounds good."

Cruz pulled forward and turned onto the mountain road that wound around to the highway. Traffic was light this time of day. Kids just home from school and workers still finishing out their days. The vehicle climbed up the side of the mountain, and he took a moment to appreciate the white-tipped evergreens and peaks of the Smoky's on the horizon. Soon enough he would be having a difficult conversation with a woman he'd never met and another he couldn't get out of his head.

The on ramp to the highway loomed ahead, and he veered to the right, following the curve and merging onto the road. Mill Hollow settled in the dip of a valley, and Cruz pressed on the brake to slow as he joined the traffic coasting down the mountain.

The car didn't slow.

"What the hell?" He pressed harder, but still nothing happened. The cruiser picked up speed as it traveled downhill.

"What's wrong?" Alarm sparked in Zoe's voice, and she glanced around.

"The brakes." He stomped his foot as hard as he could on the pedal. "They aren't working." Panic surged high in Cruz's gut, like he was plunging down the first hill of a rollercoaster. But this wasn't an amusement ride. The fall of the hill ahead showed a twist in the road and oncoming headlights. Cruz white-knuckled the steering wheel. Whipping through his mind every scenario that could save them and coming up empty. If he didn't think of something fast, they'd both be dead.

14

"What do you mean the brakes don't work?" Zoe pushed her foot against the floor as if she could make the car stop herself. She darted her gaze around her, taking in the vehicles they passed as the car continued to gain speed.

"I don't know. The brakes aren't working." Cruz's voice was calm and steady, but the firm set of his jaw and tension of his shoulders screamed out his fear.

Zoe molded her body against the seat, her hand gripping the handle inside the door. The scenery whizzed by in a blur. "What are we supposed to do?" She shrieked out the question, not wanting to know the answer.

Cruz jerked the wheel to the side, nearly clipping the back of an SUV. "I have to figure out how to stop the damn car." He hissed out the statement through gritted teeth, his grip tight on the wheel.

Her mind spun quicker than the turning tires speeding down the highway. She closed her eyes, blocking out the terrifying reality unfolding around her, willing her brain to come up with a plan.

"Damnit." Cruz barked out the word, swerving again, blaring the horn as he moved.

Her body whipped with the sudden motion, and her eyes shot open. Speeding along in the fast lane of the two-laned highway, the view from the driver's side boasted the tips of trees as they cascaded down the mountain. She glanced out her window. Craggy bushes sprouted along the rusted guardrail surrounding the rocky edges of the peak. Her stomach dropped.

Neither a great option for crashing a car, but she'd rather risk her luck with the jagged rocks.

She focused out the window, searching for anything that could stop their downward momentum with the least amount of danger.

"I'm going to switch to the inside lane and put on my hazard lights," Cruz yelled over the horn still blaring.

She leaned as far forward as her taut seatbelt allowed. The car drifted to the lane away from the steep drop off down the mountain. "Does the emergency brake work?"

Cruz licked his lips, concentration pulling the lines in around his mouth tight. "Should, but I need to slow the car first if possible. If I use the emergency brake while going this fast, it could cause us to spin out or flip the car."

Better than crashing down the side of the mountain.

She kept her thoughts to herself. She didn't have a better plan, and she trusted Cruz. Casting doubt wouldn't help anyone right now. Licking her lips, she considered the guardrail that separated the brim of the road from the rocky side of the mountain. "What about the railing? If you skim the side of the car against it, maybe it can slow us enough to use the brake." If it didn't cause them to smash against the jagged boulders of the cliff, but again, no need to state the obvious.

Gritting his teeth, Cruz veered off the shoulder and the car jostled over the uneven terrain.

Her body bounced up and down, and she squeezed the door handle. The tires rolled over a thin strip of grass, coming closer and closer to the metal railing.

"Brace yourself." Cruz tapped the passenger side of the cruiser against the guardrail blocking the mountain.

Metal screeched against metal and the windows shook, the speed of the car slowing slightly. Cars whizzed by, some slowing as they passed. Her heart lodged in her throat, fear pitching higher than the darkening sky.

"You okay?" Cruz asked.

"As okay as I can be." She cringed as the front fender brushed against the railing another time and tightened every muscle in her body, waiting for disaster to strike. Her nerves screamed and she clenched her teeth so hard her jaw ached.

"I need to skim along the side of the railing more. Before the curve in the road ahead."

Cruz edged the car closer, and the sound of metal scraping against the door rattled her teeth. Nails on a chalkboard didn't hold a candle to the ungodly noise at her side, as if the railing would burst through the door at any second. Her body shook and she held her breath, but the car slowed little by little. The bend in the road approached at an alarming rate, and Zoe braced for impact—either spinning out into traffic or smashing against the side of a mountain.

"I'm going to pull the emergency brake now!" Cruz yelled over the noise, warning her.

She closed her eyes, not wanting to see the outcome. The car screeched and slid forward, the sound of the sudden shift of gears heavy and foreboding. The halting motion slammed her body forward. The guardrail scrapped against the car. Her neck screamed as her head snapped like the end of a whip. The car swung to the side, and the passenger side of the car crashed against something hard. Her body jerked toward Cruz and the center console jabbed into her ribs. Pain exploded inside her, stars dominating the blackness of her vision, before she was tossed back into her seat and the car skidded to a stop.

A seatbelt clicked through the eerie silence and urgent hands skimmed over her arms, her face. "Zoe. Are you okay?"

Chancing a peek, she stared into Cruz's clear blue eyes. Blood dotted a cut on his forehead. Reaching out, she touched the tender flesh around the wound. "You're bleeding."

He winced then covered her fingers with his, bringing their joined hands down on her lap. "Just a small cut. I'm fine. But what about you? Are you hurt?"

She took mental stock of her body. Her muscles ached and her neck was sore, but other than that, she was fine. "Not one scratch." She managed a small smile for his benefit.

"We need to get out of the car. Can you climb over to the driver's side? The passenger door is pretty wedged against the rail."

She glanced to her side and a lead ball dropped low in her stomach. Jagged edges of brown rock pressed against the window, the door dented in and mangled. She was lucky the outcome hadn't been so much worse. "Let's go."

Keeping his fingers entwined with hers, he cupped a palm under her elbow as he backed through the driver's door and guided her to her feet. The sound of passing cars rang in her ears, but they drove by in a blur. Close enough to make Zoe nervous, yet still far enough from the narrow shoulder where they stood not to pummel into them. As soon as she found stable ground, she fell into Cruz, all the terror exploding from her in ragged breaths and an onslaught of tears.

Cruz wrapped his arms around her and held her close. He rubbed a small circle around her back and pressed his lips to her temple. "We're okay. Everything's okay."

For the first time, she didn't believe him. Not because she didn't trust him, but because they were dealing with someone a lot more dangerous than she'd realized. The man they were after wasn't just a rapist, he was a killer.

Or at least tried to be. And he'd gone after a police officer.

She shuddered. Death had come so close, and in that moment when she'd been unsure how things would end, only one thought played on repeat in her mind. She loved Cruz. She was *in* love with Cruz. And because of a past she couldn't control, she'd never know what it'd be like to tell him. To show him.

But just once, she wanted to forget all the things she couldn't give him. Instead, she tipped her chin and stared into those damn fiery eyes. Eyes that saw everything, and at the same time, made her feel like he only saw her.

Only wanted her.

Throwing caution to the wind whipping around them, she lifted on to her toes and pressed her lips to his. Just one taste. That's all she needed.

Cruz tensed for a minute, then molded her to his chest, lowering his head and deepening the kiss.

Excitement sparked her nerve endings, and she soaked up every single second. He tasted like salt and soda and salvation. She moved her lips against his, relishing the feel of his stubble against her chin, taking one last second to just enjoy being in his arms.

Because one moment was all she'd allow herself to have, even if it killed her.

CRUZ STOOD behind the back of the ambulance, the doors wide open, giving him a clear view of Zoe sitting on the gurney as an EMT checked her over. His head spun, but not from what he'd expect after finding his brake line cut and almost crashing his car into the side of a mountain. No, his near-death experience wasn't what nearly knocked him on his ass. It was the way Zoe had tucked herself seamlessly in his arms, her mouth a perfect fit against his.

Now, after a flurry of emergency vehicles had sped to their rescue, tearing into the mounting desire spiraling between him and Zoe, he was left with more questions about what to do about his feelings for Zoe than about the person responsible for tampering with his car.

Definitely not the head space he needed to be in, but damnit, how could he not when the taste of her lips was still so fresh in his mind?

Lincoln shook hands with the tow truck driver that had hooked up Cruz's totaled cruiser then sauntered over to his brother's side.

Cruz watched the tow truck pull away, his ruined car trailing behind it. He released a long breath and leaned forward, bracing the backs of his forearms on his thighs.

A heavy hand came down on his shoulder. "Did you get yourself checked out?" Lincoln's tight voice told Cruz more about what his brother felt than anything Lincoln would ever say out loud.

Cruz sniffed back all the boiling emotions threatening to explode from his skin and straightened. He needed to be strong—in control. "I'm fine. The scratch on my forehead is superficial. I'm more worried about Zoe."

Lincoln peered past him and glanced into the back of the ambulance. "You doing okay in there?"

Zoe rolled back her shoulders. "Just a little stiff."

A bit of tension in Cruz's chest loosened. No cuts or marks were evident on Zoe's body after the crash, but that didn't mean she hadn't been injured.

"Good to hear," Lincoln said.

Zoe scooted off the gurney, and Cruz hurried to offer her a hand to help her down. Once on the ground, she slipped her hand from his and tugged the open sides of her jacket together.

Cruz ignored the sting of rejection and shoved his hands in the pockets of his trousers. Discussing what had happened between them in front of Lincoln was the last thing they needed, so he couldn't blame her for pulling away. Hell, he didn't even know if he wanted anything to happen with Zoe, so why should he care if she didn't want to hold his hand?

Okay, that wasn't true. His heart screamed at him to forget his dipshit brother and finish what they'd started.

"How did this happen?" Zoe asked, breaking into his thoughts.

"Someone cut the brake line." Lincoln growled.

"Guy has balls, I'll give him that. Brakes were fine when I pulled into the Chill N' Grill. He had to work quick, in daylight, with high chances of getting caught."

Zoe furrowed her brow. "How long were you there before I arrived?"

Cruz shrugged. "Not long. Maybe ten minutes."

"Someone would have to really know their way around cars to get it done that fast. Didn't that Mike guy own an autobody shop?" Lincoln asked.

"Mike the guy I went on one date with?" Zoe shook her head, frowning, then took a step further from the road as a car whizzed by. "I thought you already talked to him?"

Cruz angled his body to shield Zoe from the oncoming traffic. "I did, and nothing set my internal alarm off. But I could have been wrong." He shoved a hand through his hair, hating that he might have looked past the bastard responsible for terrorizing them. "But even for a guy with a vast knowledge of cars, ten minutes isn't much time at all. He would have had to cut my brake line and be out of sight before Zoe pulled into the parking lot."

"I didn't notice anyone when I got there, but I wasn't paying much attention."

Lincoln ran fingers over his scraggly beard. "Maybe he waited until you were both inside. Followed Zoe to the bar then seized an opportunity."

"Followed me from the retreat?" Her eyes widened, and she glanced at Cruz. "I ran into Dusty when you called. Do you think he followed me when I left?"

Anger boiled in his gut. "I'm not sure, but you can bet I'll find out. When we get back into town, I need to get Wade's security footage and then have a talk with Dusty. Then we need to have someone go over your car with a fine-tooth comb."

Fear dilated Zoe's pupils. "You think he messed with my car?"

"Better safe than sorry," Lincoln chimed in. "Chances are he only had enough time to hit one car, and he has no reason to want *you* dead. He wants Cruz away from you. What better way than killing him, or at the very least causing a bad enough accident to put him in the hospital?"

The EMT who treated Zoe closed the back of his truck and waved. "I'm heading out. Both of you should take it easy. Over the counter pain medications or a hot soak in a tub could help with those sore muscles."

"Thanks, Ted," Cruz said with a dip of his chin. "Appreciate it."

"Yes, thank you." Zoe unwrapped her arms from around her body and lifted a hand before returning to her earlier pose.

"I can give you guys a ride into town." Lincoln dug into his jacket pocket for his keys.

"Thanks, man."

"You can take us home after we speak to Lexi," Zoe said, brows raised.

Cruz stared at her, mouth gaping. "Are you serious?"

She tilted her head to the side, that stubborn set of her lips he knew all too well firmly in place. "Does it look like I'm joking?"

Lincoln chuckled, then covered his mouth with the back of his hand when Cruz shot him a glare.

"Lexi will be there tomorrow." Cruz tried to keep his voice as calm as possible. When Zoe had her mind made up, it was nearly impossible to get her to see things differently. "She'll understand why we had to postpone."

"And who knows what else will happen to me tomorrow —to you? I don't want to wait any longer than necessary to get answers. Do you?"

"No, but—"

"But nothing," Zoe said, then turned to Lincoln. "Can you drive us to Mill Hollow before we head back to Pine Valley?"

Lincoln turned an amused smirk toward Cruz then smiled at Zoe. "Sure thing, boss. Let's get going."

Cruz bit his tongue, refusing to argue with either one of them when he knew damn well it'd be a losing fight. Instead, he stormed over to Lincoln's car, whipped open the passenger door, and waited for Zoe to get settled inside before cramming his long legs in the backseat. His muscles screamed and his head throbbed, but it was his heart that kept him on edge.

Because even though there were a hundred reasons why he couldn't be with Zoe, he couldn't stop replaying that kiss. No way in hell he could go the rest of his life without tasting Zoe at least one more time.

15

Zoe released a long breath before stepping out of Lincoln's car and onto the sidewalk in front of Plentiful Pages Bookshop. A slap of wind nearly dropped her back down on the seat. Her movements were stiff and jerky. A dull thud pulsed over most of her body. She yearned to slip into a hot bath then crawl under her covers and fade away into a dreamless sleep.

But that wasn't an option right now. She needed to talk to Lexi Myer. She needed answers.

Cruz hurried to her side and a flash of pain skittered across his face for just a beat. He glanced up and down the quaint, downtown street with its brick sidewalks and mom and pop stores flanking the road, probably making sure a psychopath wasn't waiting nearby to pounce. "You up for this?"

She nodded. "Now's as good a time as any." Wanting to get this over with, she forged ahead of Lincoln and Cruz and opened the door to the little shop nestled inside the white-washed stone building.

A bell jingled above the door. Warmth welcomed Zoe

inside the store, and it wasn't just from the heat blasting from overhead vents. The space was like walking into a warm hug. Red, exposed brick covered the walls and dark, scarred floorboards ran the length of the room. Mismatched rugs covered patches of open space and were tucked under random chairs and places to sit with a book. Shelves crammed together, each section announced by a handmade sign hanging from the ceiling.

A soft meow grabbed Zoe's attention, and she knelt as a calico kitten strolled her way, tail twitching and curiosity bright in his yellow eyes. "Well, hello there, little one." Zoe held out a hand for the kitten to rub against.

"I see you've met Oliver, resident greeter." A tall, slender woman emerged from the back of the store with a friendly smile on her face. Her long, auburn hair fell in loose waves around her shoulders. Her black cigarette pants and olive-green turtleneck made her look like she belonged in a trendy café spouting poetry instead of a small-town bookstore.

The cat meowed then ran to the woman, who bent to scoop him into her arms before straightening. "Welcome," she said. "Can I help you find anything?"

Cruz stepped forward. "We're here to speak with Lexi Myer."

Her smile slipped, probably put off by the two uniformed officers, one with a nasty cut across his forehead. "I'm Lexi."

Cruz extended a hand. "I'm Officer Cruz Sawyer, and this is my brother, Officer Lincoln Sawyer."

Lincoln waited for Lexi to shake Cruz's hand, then offered his own and gave a hearty shake. "Thanks for agreeing to talk with us."

Lexi nodded at Lincoln then turned her attention on

Zoe. "You must be the woman attacked this week that I was told about. I'm sorry. I'll do whatever I can to help."

Unable to speak, Zoe nodded. She couldn't tear her gaze from Lexi's auburn hair. She pinched the ends of her own hair, the color so similar to Lexi's, and cringed as memories of her attacker crashed into her. Him on top of her, slashing his knife through her thick strands before pressing the sharp blade to her neck. Her throat constricted, and she coughed to expel the emotion making it hard to swallow.

Mirroring Zoe's movement, Lexi grazed the bottom of her own hair with her index finger. "Did he cut off a piece of your hair, too?" She asked, as if reading Zoe's thoughts. Her voice wobbled, and she settled her hand on the top of the kitten's head.

"Yes." The word barely squeezed from her tight throat.

Cruz clenched his jaw. "You both have similar hair color, and if he's taken strands of it as a sick trophy of some kind, it has to mean something."

"Agreed," Lincoln said.

Bile rumbled in Zoe's gut. She pressed her hands to her stomach, trying to squash the queasiness. "Do you have any idea who did this to you? A gut instinct the police couldn't pin down? A suspicion that never panned out?"

Lexi shrugged. "Not really. The police looked into everyone I could think of from my past, as well as people I came into contact with every day. Hell, they even grilled my boyfriend. Like he'd break into my store and rape me when we'd been together for two years."

"Boyfriend?" Cruz asked, brow furrowed. "Might explain why your attacker came to your store. Was there ever any evidence someone broke into your home?"

"A few weird things stood out, but nothing concrete.

Especially in a home with two people coming and going. My boyfriend and I moved in together shortly before this happened. So if a window was left unlocked or something moved from its normal place, we couldn't always say for sure it wasn't us. We hadn't paid attention to those things in the early days. We were just so happy to have taken that step." A dreamy-eyed stare chased away the pain and sadness from her green eyes.

A twinge of jealousy made Zoe's heart shudder, and she hated herself for it. Here was a strong woman who'd been through hell—who'd been attacked at her place of business in a way Zoe had thankfully avoided—and she was jealous because the woman had a boyfriend who lived with her? Could she be any pettier?

She cut her gaze to Cruz, and her cheeks heated. Her pathetic need to feel close to Cruz had led her to act rashly. What the hell had she been thinking when she planted that kiss on him?

"Are you still with your boyfriend?" Zoe couldn't help but ask the question. A part of her wanted to know someone who'd been through the same nightmare as her could end up happy.

"It was touch and go for a while, but we worked through it and will be married soon."

Zoe glanced at the woman's hand and smiled at the glittering diamond.

Cruz cleared his throat. "The officer who handled your case gave me a list of suspects questioned, and none of them were familiar to Zoe," he said, crashing into the fleeting moment of positive conversation.

"How can you be sure it's the same guy?" Lexi set the cat on the floor then crossed her arms over her chest.

"We can't," Lincoln said. "But we have a better under-standing of that now. You two have such similar hair colors and the attacker sheared strands off from you both. Odds aren't high we're looking at two different men."

The bell jingled again, and Zoe jumped.

Lexi lifted her mouth into another smile and waved at the customer. "Welcome. Come get me if you need help. I'll be in the back." She nodded toward the rear of the store. "Can we talk back here?"

Zoe followed behind Lexi, Cruz and Lincoln behind her, until they reached the distressed counter with an antique register propped on top.

Lexi scooted behind the counter and rested her tightly clasped hands on the weathered wood. "Look, I'll tell you anything you'd like to know. Rehash the entire, terrible night. But I don't know what else I can tell you that could make a difference. Especially if you've talked to Officer Douglas. She was thorough, and I know it eats her up she never nailed whoever did this."

Her words were a low blow to Zoe, and she hunched her shoulders forward. Really, what had she expected? She'd come here and ask a couple questions and everything would click into place—the man that alluded them at every turn would magically show up?

"What about a smell?" Zoe asked, turning the question over in her mind. Both times her attacker had held her to him, spoke close to her face, the same scent wafted from his warm breath. The scent was common, and probably didn't mean anything, but it could be one more link binding her with Lexi.

Lexi connected her gaze with Zoe, her delicate jawline locked tight. "Peppermint. I can't smell it now or I get sick. The asshole smelled like peppermint."

PAIN SPIKED between Cruz's eyes, and he fought the urge to let his eyelids drift closed and fall asleep into a blessed oblivion. Night had fallen hours before. After speaking with Lexi, Lincoln had swung by Cruz's place so he and Zoe could gather their things then drop them off at the retreat. Now, he sat in a kitchen that looked almost exactly like the one in Brooke's cabin and listened to the sound of water rushing from the shower.

If he thought Zoe sleeping across the hall from him was torture, that was nothing compared to sitting and imagining her wet and naked under a warm spray of water only fifteen feet away. Not to mention the taste of her lips still embedded into his head.

He cupped his palms around a cold bottle of beer, half the bitter liquid already gone. His nerves were shot, and he jiggled his leg up and down, unable to keep it steady. Thoughts and questions ricocheted around his mind, bouncing between his near-accident on the side of a mountain, his mind-blowing kiss with Zoe, and what he'd learned from their conversation with Lexi.

Not like he needed to speak with Lexi Myer to know whoever was responsible for what happened to her was the same one who was after Zoe. One look was all it took. The long, auburn hair. The striking green eyes and tall, slender builds. The two women looked like they could be related, and that had to mean something.

His phone vibrated on the table beside him, jolting him back to the present. He swiped the screen to life and answered the call. "Cruz here."

"Hey Cruz, it's Isaac."

Cruz searched the unfamiliar space for a clock. The IT

specialist would have been off the clock hours before. "Hey, man. What's up?"

"Sorry it took so long, but I finally got that footage you brought into the station cleaned up. At least, as cleaned up as I can manage. I can't tell what's in the guy's hand when he breaks into Zoe's studio, but it definitely looks like it's attached to his keyring. I'm sending it your way now so you can take a look. Maybe you'll have better luck figuring out what it is."

The phone vibrated again, and he hit the speaker button before opening the picture. "Got it. Thanks." Squinting, he held the screen close to his face. "What the hell is that?" A grainy black and white image showed a closeup from the security footage. Strands of feathers or thread bunched together like a tassel of some kind.

"Almost looks like one of those things high school graduates wear on their caps," Isaac said.

"You're right. But why would a grown man carry that around?" Unless the man they were after was much younger than he'd assumed. "I appreciate you working late and getting this over to me."

"Any time. Let me know if there's anything else I can do."

Cruz disconnected the call but kept his focus on the picture, trying to decipher what exactly he was looking at.

Footsteps padded the ground behind him, and the warmth of Zoe's body heated his back. "What are you looking at?" She leaned down from behind the chair and brought her cheek so close he had to fight his urge to turn to the side, grab her face, and pick up where they left off on the side of the road. She gasped and moved within inches of his phone. "Is that hair?"

He tightened his grip on the hard plastic case as the reality of her words sunk in. "Holy shit. You're right. This sick sonofabitch is taking hair from his victims, and not just keeping it, but carrying it around with him."

"Oh my God. I'm going to get sick."

Cruz shut off the screen and hurried to his feet. He cupped a palm under Zoe's elbow and led her to the couch. "It's all right. I've got you." He eased her down then took the space beside her, hovering on the edge of the cushion in case she needed him to grab anything.

"This madness has to stop. How can this guy walk around all this time with no one the wiser? Lexi was raped close to a year ago. How many other women has he tortured? How many more does he watch, waiting to strike?" Her cheeks were still flushed from her shower, but the rest of her skin paled. Drips of water leaked from the ends of her hair and soaked her purple tank top.

Cruz skimmed his knuckles up and down the gentle slope of her bicep, wanting to comfort her but not wanting to get too close—to touch too much exposed skin. His self-control was on a very thin leash, and caressing her soft, dewy flesh had him at the brink of losing it. "We will stop him. I promise."

She lifted her hands then let them drop onto her lap. "How? We have hardly anything working in our favor. Not one little break in the case. How will we put a stop to this?"

"I know it's hard to see, but we're making progress." He moved his hand up and down, swallowing hard as lust sparked in his core. Not trusting himself, he kept his gaze locked on her eyes. Unwilling to take in the rest of her body, still warm and damp from the shower. "There's the hair, your resemblance to Lexi, and the fact this guy knows his way around cars. Lincoln's checking out Dusty and Mike's alibis, and tomorrow, we'll press harder. Look deeper into any connections with Lexi. Something has to be there we aren't seeing."

Tears filled Zoe's eyes then rolled down her cheeks.

Cruz's resolve crumbled. He wrapped his arm around her shoulders and crushed her against him. His heart thudded like a herd of stallions in his chest. He snaked his hand through her wet strands, cradling the back of her head.

A sob hitched in Zoe's throat. Burying her face in his neck, she fisted his t-shirt in her hand. "I can't keep living like this. Afraid of my own shadow. Always watching my back and wondering if I'm paranoid for feeling like someone is watching me. I just want to go back to the way things were."

Her statement slammed against him. "Do you want *everything* to go back to the way things were?" The question came out before he could stop it. Damnit, now wasn't the time to discuss their kiss. He wasn't even sure he wanted to explore what had happened.

Her soft sigh brushed against his skin, and she pulled back to face him. "Most of it, yeah. But what you're talking about..." she licked her lips as her gaze dropped to his mouth. "That kiss was impulsive. I was terrified and just acted."

"Do you regret it?"

She connected her wide eyes with his. "No."

Warmth exploded in his chest, running down until it heated his entire being. "I don't either. But I don't know if it should happen again. I can't promise you a future, Zoe."

Lifting a hand, she traced his mouth with the pad of her thumb, her gaze following the motion. "I didn't say a word about the future. Right now, in this moment, I just don't want to think. I don't want to be afraid. I just want to be happy...with you."

A flurry of ideas penetrated his thoughts—all things he could do to make Zoe happy. To take her mind far away from reality for just one night. "Are you sure? I don't want anything to ruin our friendship. You mean too damn much to me."

She lifted her gaze then pressed her finger to his mouth. "No more talking." Slowly, she moved forward and nibbled on his lip.

He moaned and pushed his hands further into her hair. Tilting his head, he pulled his lip from her teeth then dove in, devouring her mouth with his. She parted her lips and he slipped his tongue inside her, tasting her.

Needing to be closer, to be touching more of her, he circled one arm around the small of her back and hooked the other under her knees, bringing her to sit on his lap.

Giggling, she shifted, straddling him.

His head spun as her heat encased him. She was fucking captivating. He crushed her mouth to his again, his tongue diving deeper, harder than before. He wanted to taste her. All of her.

She writhed against him, her body slow and in a steady rhythm, the friction of their clothes increasing the incredible torture until he couldn't take it any longer.

Breaking away, he struggled to catch his breath. He had to make sure she wanted this...*really* wanted this. "Zoe. Are you sure?"

She halted the motion of her hips and rested her palm against his cheek. Her lips were swollen and red. "Hell yes. I want you, Cruz Sawyer, and I want you now."

That's all he needed to hear. Scooping her into his arms like a groom carrying a bride, he dotted kisses along her jawline and up her neck as he carried her to bed. He committed the feel of her in his arms to memory, relishing the taste of her skin and the smell of the still-fresh soap. Tonight he would put his past behind him and give all of himself to this woman he loved.

16

A twinge of guilt tightened Zoe's grip on her new set of keys as she unlocked the door to her studio the next morning. Between a night of mind-blowing acrobatics with Cruz and the terrifying car accident, her sore muscles begged to be stretched. Then there was her heart. She'd needed some space after the intimacy she and Cruz had experienced. The sex was great, but the emotional connection she'd felt was so raw and intense, it'd left her stomach churning—her mind racing.

No one had ever made her feel all the feels the way Cruz had, and that knowledge had her sneaking out of bed before daybreak. He'd told her he couldn't give her a future, and she'd jumped in bed without another thought. She had nothing to offer him either, but their kiss had been electrifying. She *needed* to know what a night in Cruz's bed would be like.

She pushed open the door and flipped on the lights. Anxiety shook her hands. Now that she knew what she'd been missing, she had to evaluate what that meant for their friendship. In order to do that, she couldn't wake up beside him and get swept away in a stupid fantasy that would never come true. She could never be a whole woman, which meant she couldn't saddle a man like Cruz with a future that couldn't provide him with all the things he may one day want.

Luckily, Brooke had been awake when she'd called and agreed to come into town with her. Zoe might need space from Cruz right now, but she wasn't stupid. No way she'd open her studio alone. Turning the deadbolt from its place, she swung the door wide for Brooke to enter.

"Thank you much." Brooke hurried inside. "Is Tasha coming in today?"

Zoe stepped across the threshold, closing and locking the door behind them. She couldn't afford to cancel class today, but she'd be smart about it. She'd keep the door locked until classes began, then see every person out and put the deadbolt back in place when they left. Life couldn't stay at a standstill when bills needed paid. Her savings was modest and couldn't carry her more than a couple of months if she stopped classes until this nightmare was over.

Zoe inhaled a deep breath and took in the comforting sight of her studio. The last couple of days felt like a lifetime. Standing in a space that was like home to her loosened the constant knot in her gut by a fraction. The familiar hum of the fluorescent lights lifted her lips. "No. I told her to take a few days off. I'm not sure what the week will bring, and I might need to cancel more classes."

Brooke shrugged out of her coat and draped it over one of the two chairs positioned in front of the window. "You should have canceled today. What did Cruz say about keeping your Mommy and Me class?"

Heat poured through her body at Cruz's name, and she turned her back to her friend. She powered up the computer on the reception desk in the lobby, keeping her focus on the screen. "He was still asleep when I left."

"What? He's going to freak out when he wakes up and you're gone. Why didn't you tell him what you were doing?"

Brooke's high-pitched squeak confirmed Zoe's poor decision. She winced and slumped into the desk chair. "I left him a note. He'll know where I am." She was surprised he hadn't already showed up and dragged her back to their room. A part of her hated that he hadn't, wishing he'd whisk her back to the lodge and they'd pick up where they'd left off in the wee hours of the morning.

"What's that look about?" Brooke narrowed her eyes.

The computer screen flashed to life. Zoe moved the cursor over the file she needed and trained her facial features to stay as even as possible. "What look?"

"Zoe Peyton, I know *that* look." Brooke hopped to her feet and rushed the counter with a wagging finger. "Something happened between you two last night, didn't it? Finally! Tell me everything."

Zoe rolled her eyes. "I have nothing to tell you except thank you for driving me into work. You can go now." She knew Brooke wouldn't leave her alone, but she didn't want the third degree right now.

Brooke shook her head. "No way. I'm not leaving you here alone. Cruz would kill me. Are you really not going to tell me what happened last night? You know we're all rooting for you two, right?"

Zoe sighed. "The only thing anyone should be rooting for is Cruz finding whoever is after me so all our lives can get back to normal."

"But, Zoe—"

"Brooke, please. I can't have this conversation right now." All her emotions were right at the surface, waiting to break free. If that happened, there'd be no way to stop the outpouring and the flood just might swallow her whole.

A knock sounded at the door. Relieved for the interruption, Zoe fixed a smile on her face and hurried to see who had arrived. The Mommy and Me classes didn't start for another twenty minutes, and she wasn't expecting anyone else.

Leo stood outside with his nose pressed against the glass. His mom stood behind him with her hand latched on the tops of his shoulders.

Chuckling, Zoe opened the door and was almost knocked over by Leo's exuberant hug. "Hey, bud. How are you?"

Leo's mom, Sandra, stepped through the door. "He better be pretty darn good or the rest of the day will be spent with some restrictions."

Zoe glanced at the other woman. Her words were harsh, but her tone light. The small grin on her face told Zoe she wasn't serious. "Being a rascal today, huh?"

Sandra planted a fist on her hip. "He told me we were running late. That by the time we got here, there'd be no more room for us. Now I know he just wanted to get me out of the house faster."

Leo frowned, either not understanding his mom was joking or in too bad of a mood to care. "I was confused."

Zoe squeezed him tight. "Confused or not, I'm glad for extra time with my favorite boy."

Sandra twisted her lips to the side. "I hate to be a pest. We can wait next door. I should have asked Brian about the time. He had to go into work last minute, and I never thought to get more information about the class. I haven't been in so long."

"It's totally fine," Zoe said with a smile. "I'm glad to see you. We can catch up and put Leo to work setting out the mats."

The boy brightened a little at the suggestion. "I can help?"

"Sure! Brooke can help you, right Brooke?" Perfect, she could keep her friend busy so she'd stop prying into the one topic she didn't want to discuss.

Brooke strolled over. She smirked, hands on hips. "Want to race me to the corner of the room where Zoe keeps the mats?"

Leo beamed and took off at a sprint.

Brooke laughed and trailed after him, slowing her pace to stay behind him. "You're too fast for me!"

Sandra sighed, drawing Zoe's attention. "Sorry about this. He's been in such a mood the last couple days. I think it's because of his dad. Then Brian had to cancel this morning, and it really set him off. Little boys don't understand that when the candy factory calls, uncles must go. We're lucky my brother can work from home as much as he does. He spends so much time with Leo."

"That's nice." She turned and watched Leo struggle to drag three yoga mats across the floor then faced Sandra again. "Wait, Brian works at a candy factory? Doesn't really fit my image of him."

"He's no Willy Wonka, that's for sure." Sandra snorted then ran a hand through her pulled-back blonde hair. "He's an accountant—though I never understood why. He was so good at working with his hands. But some big problem came up, and he had to go in and fix it. He hated disappointing Leo, but I'm sure he'll make it up in some big way. He always does. Movie passes to his favorite cinema twenty miles out of the way just because they have the best snacks, story time two towns over, he even took him to this theater series every week for month. Leo just loves being Uncle Brian's buddy. Leo would do anything for him."

Zoe rolled up her mat and laid it at her feet. The idea of Brian taking his nephew all over the place in order to cheer him up pinched Zoe's heart. When she'd been young and sad about the absence of her parents, her ma had done the same thing. Tried a hundred different activities and hobbies in an attempt to cheer Zoe up and distract her from her pain. "Leo's lucky to have such a sweet uncle."

"We both are lucky to have him around. And Leo was a bright spot for Brian after his wife died. We've all really leaned on each other."

Sadness turned down Zoe's mouth. So much loss and heartbreak. She wished her family was still around and as supportive as Sandra and her brother. But Brooke's laughter across the room reminded her that family didn't have to be blood.

Sandra scrunched her nose, and a wariness narrowed her eyes. "He talks about you sometimes."

"Leo?"

Shaking her head, Sandra chuckled. "Leo talks about you all the time, but Brian mentions how good you are with Leo. How much you give him extra attention and always make him laugh. Thank you for that. Those laughs aren't easy to come by. Sounds like you'll make a great mother one day."

The earlier pinch in her heart turned into a fist, squeezing until the pain almost brought her to her knees. She forced a smile, not wanting Sandra to understand the intended compliment was more of a sucker punch. "Thanks. How about we help your son get the studio ready?"

Zoe hurried over to the smattering of mats across the floor, straightening them. She was wrong—she couldn't just go on with business as usual. Not with so many emotions boiling right at the surface. She glanced at the clock hanging on the wall. Only ten more minutes until class started, forty more until it was over and she could cancel classes for the rest of the day. Then she could hide back at her room in the lodge, burrow under the covers, and nurse her crumbling heart.

~

CRUZ WADDED UP the note Zoe had left on the kitchen table in his fist. Seriously? They'd spent an incredible night together and she just took off? He'd woken when sunlight danced into the room, hope rising with him for the first time since Diana died.

For the first time in five years, he'd held a woman in his arms and never wanted it to end. Maybe...just maybe...he could give his heart to another woman and trust things would be different.

But then he reached for her and came up with nothing but cold sheets. Anger flared hot inside him. Damnit, he wasn't just some one-night stand. He was Zoe's friend. Had been for years. Taking a deep breath, he tampered his misplaced anger. He'd told Zoe he couldn't give her a future, so how could he blame her for bolting?

Fear coated his gut. She'd gone to open the studio this morning. If she was in town—even if she was with Brooke—there was no telling what danger waited for her. Regardless of what happened between them last night, he had a duty to protect her. And he couldn't protect her if she ran away from him.

Grabbing clothes from the duffel he'd brought and hadn't unpacked, he dressed quickly. He needed out of the room that still smelled like Zoe. The scent of her would intoxicate him, and he needed to focus on his plan for the rest of the day. He wouldn't force her to talk about last night, but he would stay glued to her side until her stalker was caught. No matter how uncomfortable it might make her.

He shut the door behind him and scurried to the kitchen. Breakfast had already been served, but he needed food. And not the nasty shit Brooke stocked for the guests. He knew her trick—keeping the good stuff at the lodge to lure her guests out of the private spaces.

He raked a hand through his hair as he crossed through the lobby. What he really needed was Zoe. He could wring her neck for leaving without him—without even waking him and telling him her plans. But more than that, although he was hurt, all he wanted was to drive to the studio, bring her back to the bed they'd shared, and not let her out for the next two days.

He entered the kitchen and slowed to a crawl at the sound of bickering.

Chet stood with his huge arms folded across his chest staring at a woman in front of the stove. "Don't burn it again. What the hell was Brooke thinking hiring you?"

The woman spun on her heels, her tight, black curls bouncing around her face, and pointed the tip of her spatula at Chet. "She was thinking *you* need help. Which you do. Stop complaining."

"Sorry to interrupt." Cruz took another step inside the kitchen, unsure of what he'd just walked in on.

Chet growled and shot him a quick glance before returning his focus to the small woman. "Get what you want."

"Thanks." Cruz made a beeline for the refrigerator and studied its contents. He wasn't too hungry, but fuel was necessary to get his day started. A clear plastic wrap covered a platter, and he pulled it out.

"Would you stop?" the woman said through clenched teeth. "I can feel you breathing down my neck. I know what I'm doing."

Chet snorted. "Really? The candy lady knows how to cook. How rich."

The tension in the room had Cruz grabbing an egg sandwich from the platter then putting the platter back where he'd found it. "I'll just eat this cold."

"Sorry," Chet said.

"Oh, so he does know how to apologize." The woman cocked a hip and fire flew from her narrowed gaze before she turned a smile on Cruz. "Hi. I'm Mia. The new kitchen help."

Chet worked his jaw back and forth.

Clarity brought the situation into focus, and sympathy for both Chet and Mia flooded him. Having someone come in and replace Chet's murdered cousin had to be hard as hell. And for Mia, stepping into the shoes of someone Chet had lost so tragically was a tough spot. Hoping to diffuse a bit of tension, Cruz returned Mia's smile. "Nice to meet you. I'm Cruz Sawyer."

"Are you a guest here?"

"He's one of Pine Valley's finest," Chet said. "Not a guest."

"I'm staying in a room at the lodge for work. Hopefully for just a couple of nights." He took a bite of the sandwich and cringed. He really should have zapped it in the microwave.

"Anything new on Zoe's case?" Chet turned his back to Mia, as if trying to keep her out of the conversation.

"Not really. I'm about to call Lincoln for a ride to the

station. We have a few strings to tug on this morning."
Lincoln had texted that both Dusty and Mike claimed alibis
for the timeframe when Cruz's car had been tampered with,
but neither could prove it. Both men needed questioned
further.

Chet nodded then aimed his irritated gaze back on Mia.
"The edges are burnt. Throw it away."

Mia shook her head, mumbling something under her
breath as she slid whatever was in the pan into the trash.

"See you guys around." Cruz backed out of the kitchen,
not envying Mia. Chet's gruff demeanor could be off-
putting, but the circumstances had sharpened Chet's rough
edges and made them pointy and dangerous. He hoped Mia
could stick it out.

Lincoln jogged down the hall, toward the kitchen doors.
Deep lines ran the length of his forehead and his energy
screamed something was wrong. "There you are. I've been
calling you."

Cruz patted the pockets of his jeans. Damnit, in his haste
to get out of the room, he'd left his phone behind. "What
happened?"

"I stopped by Dusty's cabin. He's gone."

17

The Mommy and Me class did nothing to put Zoe in a better head space. Her night with Cruz, anxiety over everything happening, and the weird vibe in a room that was usually full of laughter and high-spirits had put her on edge. Maybe the handful of kids could sense her strange mood, but whatever the reason, tension had pounded in Zoe's head along with every move.

"That was an interesting class," Brooke said as she wiped off the yoga mats. "Noisier than what I'm used to, but for once I felt like I was at the top of the class. Most of these kids couldn't even do a chair pose. What have you been teaching them?"

Brooke's teasing forced a laugh from Zoe. "Everything was off. Especially Leo. He's usually so happy and rambunctious. Today, he just kind of moped around, barely moving." Grabbing a piece of white paper from a drawer, she wrote 'Classes Canceled for the Day. Sorry for the Inconvenience' in large, loopy letters. She hated that people would waste time coming into town for a class that had been canceled, but she just didn't have it in her to stick it out. She'd make sure to create a post on her social media pages as well in hopes people caught the notice before heading into town.

"We all have those days. His mother seemed upset as well. She was mighty chatty when they first got here. You'll have to tell me more about this charming uncle she talked so much about." Brooke placed the last mat back in the cubby in the corner then wiped her palms on her bright blue leggings. "What's next? Is another class coming soon? I probably won't feel as good about myself if I have to do yoga with an advanced group."

Ignoring the comment about Brian, Zoe held up the sign. "You were right. This was a mistake. Shutting down for another day or two won't break the bank."

Brooke crossed the room and stopped at Zoe's side. She hooked an arm over her shoulder. "Want to punch a giant bag again?"

"Maybe." Zoe pulled in a large breath. "I can't just sit and wait. Maybe I'll go find the woman you hired to help Chet. Introduce myself."

"Great idea. She's very nice and doesn't know anyone in town. I'm sure she'd love a friend." Brooke bumped her hip against Zoe. "You are the best one around. I need to run to the bathroom really quick before we take off. You okay?"

Zoe shot Brooke an are-you-kidding-me smirk. "I think I'll be fine for a couple minutes. You pee, I'll post the sign, then we'll leave."

Brooke raised her hands in surrender. "Fine. Just checking. I'll be right back."

Zoe clucked her tongue as she rummaged around the drawers behind the front counter in search of tape. After locating what she needed, she hurried to the door and swung it wide open. The slight tint of the glass could make the notice difficult to read, so she'd have to smother it with tape on the outside of the door. She turned her back to the street and put plenty of tape on the paper. The last thing she needed was a gust of wind to send the paper blowing away.

"Zoe, can we talk?"

The husky voice slid across the back of her neck with the precision of a razor blade and lifted the hairs on her arms. She turned slowly, pressing her back to the door, and faced Dusty. She clutched the handle with a trembling hand, unsure of how to respond. "Now isn't really a good time."

He shoved a hand over the top of his head and darted his gaze up and down the deserted street. Not so much as a car drove down the road. "Well, it's the only time I've got because I'm leaving. But before I go, I wanted to clear things up with you."

She swallowed hard. "Nothing to clear up, Dusty. I wish you the best."

He fixed his wild-eyed stare on her. "Honestly, I don't know why I feel like I have to explain myself. But damnit, somehow I got caught up in the middle of this."

His words set off a siren of alarm in her head. Maybe Dusty wasn't the one they wanted, but what had brought him to her studio? And how did he know where she was? Curiosity had her relaxing her stance. "Caught in the middle of what? What did you do?"

"I didn't do anything." He shouted the words—hands fisted at his sides. Red invaded his cheeks as he fought to keep his temper in check. "But the police keep questioning me and your name was brought up. I can only assume you were told about my past. I've worked hard to be a good person, and I don't want you thinking the worst of me."

Disappointment kicked her in the gut and the fear from before swept in to take its place. The idea she needed to hear him out before leaving was beyond odd. "I don't think the worst of you. I promise." She forced a smile, trying her best to stay calm and get him to leave her alone. Slowly she slid her hand down her side toward the pocket in her leggings. Damnit, she didn't even have her phone on her.

He shook his head and kept his intense gaze locked on hers. "I moved to Tennessee for a fresh start. To leave behind a past that was chained to me like a lock without a key. But there's no getting away from what happened. There will always be someone looking into me, trying to figure out what's none of their business."

Not knowing what else to do, she opted to speak the truth. She didn't have anything to lose at this point. A truck idled at the side of the road—probably Dusty's. If he wanted to take her, he would. No one was around to stop him. "Cruz was looking for someone who hurt me. That's it. His interest in your past had nothing to do with you. Except for the fact you'd asked me to breakfast. That's it."

Dusty scrunched his face together. "What? He thought I hurt you? You thought because I wanted to eat with you, I was someone to fear?" He kicked at a stone and watched it skitter down the sidewalk. "I came here to heal. Not hurt anyone. Especially you, who's been nothing but kind. I just wanted a friend. I swear."

The drastic swing of his temperament made her uneasy. She didn't want to dance around the situation for one more second. She needed answers, then she had to get away from this man. Squaring her shoulders, she set her mouth in a firm line and laid all her cards on the table. "You didn't break into my home and attack me?"

He reared back, either genuinely surprised by her statement or a damn good actor. "No. I don't even know where you live. How would I?"

She watched his reaction, searching for signs that he was uncomfortable or lying. Finding out where she lived wouldn't be any more complicated than locating her studio. "What about the woman you forced yourself on?"

He dropped his gaze to his feet. "What happened with her was a mistake. We were drunk. Both of us."

Anger roared to life inside her. "That's not an excuse to violate another human being."

He lifted his face toward the sky. "We kissed then I got handsy. I don't remember her pushing me away or telling me no. Maybe she did." He shrugged then faced her. "I will always try to do better. Be a better man."

His statement twisted something inside her. Cruz made it sound like Dusty was adamant he hadn't hurt the woman in question, but this was something else. This was admitting that he wasn't sure what had happened, and he didn't say he was sorry or wrong. He said he'd do better. A chill swept over her. She might not know what he meant by that cryptic vow, but she knew she had to get away from him. Now. "I need to get inside."

Reaching for her, he took a step forward. "Zoe. Please. Talk to me."

Nothing about this interaction sat right with Zoe. She barely knew this man. His desire to be close to her—to know her—spoke of someone who was delusional about where their relationship stood.

Someone who could be very, very dangerous.

"Zoe? Where'd you go?" Brooke's voice called from inside the studio.

Dusty widened his eyes then turned and fled to his truck, speeding off down the road.

Brooke appeared in the doorway and frowned. "What's going on?"

Zoe hurried inside, shut the door, and twisted the lock. "Dusty was here." She watched the taillights disappear down the road and ordered her heart to stop racing. "I need to call Cruz."

~

As soon as he pulled to a stop, Cruz jumped out of Lincoln's cruiser and ran to the door of Mountain Serenity Studios. His heart had been lodged in his throat since the frantic phone call from Zoe. Not wanting her to chance leaving and being followed, he'd told her and Brooke to stay put until he could get to them.

He yanked on the door handle, but it didn't budge. Fisting his hand, he pounded on the glass barrier, needing to see for himself Zoe was all right. "Zoe! It's me! Open the door!" He shielded his eyes with his hand and peered inside.

Zoe appeared from the back of the studio and ran across the wooden floors. A deep frown pulled down her lips, and her hands shook as she turned the deadbolt and opened the door. On a sigh, she flung herself into his arms. "I shouldn't have left you like that. Should have woken you to let you know I had classes."

His injured pride at being left in an empty bed flew right out the window. His arms went around her, and he held her tight. "Everything's okay."

Lincoln cleared his throat. "Let's take this inside, shall we?"

Cruz dropped his hand to the small of Zoe's back and ushered her over the threshold. "Tell me what happened."

Zoe sucked in a deep breath and waited for Brooke to cross the room to Lincoln's side before she began. "I was outside putting up a sign to cancel class, and Dusty just showed up. He kept saying how he needed me to understand he wasn't a bad guy. That he hadn't done anything to hurt me. When I asked him about the woman he'd forced himself on, he admitted he didn't remember what really happened. Said he'd do better next time."

"Did he touch you at all? Hurt you?" Red invaded Cruz's vision. For a man who claimed to not have any previous knowledge of Zoe, he seemed to appear out of nowhere a lot. And why would he feel the need to prove himself to a woman he'd just met? What was the point if he'd never see her again?

Zoe wrapped her arms around herself and shook her head.

Lincoln glanced at Brooke. "Did he let you know he was leaving?"

"I haven't heard anything, but he might have left a message at the front desk. Whoever is working this morning wouldn't have notified me if someone checked out early. It happens sometimes, and there's never any reason for concern."

"You should call and find out," Lincoln said. "If he's all checked out then we can go in his cabin and search for anything he might have left behind. No warrant needed."

Brooke linked her hand in his and tilted her head toward the small waiting room to their side. "My phone's in my coat pocket. Why don't you come with me while I make the call?"

Lincoln narrowed his eyes but followed behind Brooke without a word.

When they were out of ear shot, Cruz faced Zoe. "Are you sure you're okay?"

Licking her lips, she nodded. "I mean, Dusty didn't lay a hand on me. He just rattled me—showing up like that out of

the blue. Then with everything that happened last night..."
She shrugged and refused to meet his eyes.

Disappointment squeezed his chest. He might have
woken up filled with hope, but he'd told Zoe he couldn't
give her a future right before he'd taken her to bed. No
wonder she'd fled with the morning light. He'd given her no
reason to stay. Tucking his thumb under her chin, he forced
her to look at him. "Last night was amazing."

A light blush stained her cheeks. "It was."

"I'm sorry if I gave you the wrong impression."

She widened her gaze for a moment then took a step
away. "You didn't. You made your intentions perfectly clear."

Shit. That's not what he meant. His words bumbled
along on his tongue like he was an idiot. It'd been so long
since he'd had to confess his feelings to a woman that he
was messing it all up. "No. That's not what I meant."

A sad smile lifted her lips. "It's fine. We're consenting
adults, and we both understood what last night was."

Inching closer, he tilted his head to study her. Maybe
before he laid his heart at her feet, he should hear her
thoughts on the matter. He'd assumed they were on the
same page—that he had made her feel things she'd never
felt before just like she had done to him. But maybe he was
mistaken. "And what was it?"

She shrugged. "A chance to forget all the chaos for a
little while. To just let go of all my fears and worries for one
second. Last night was wonderful, and you made me so
happy. But we both knew that it was a one-time thing. You
were right, there is no future for us. At least not like that."
Her smile tightened. "We're friends. Good friends."

Her statement sucked the air from his lungs, but he
couldn't let her see how much she'd hurt him. Blindsided
him. She was right. They were friends, and if he wanted to

keep her in his life, he couldn't let her know how far he'd fallen for her. Returning her smile with one of his own, he dipped his chin. "Glad we're on the same page. Now we can focus on why Dusty stopped here this morning. The whole thing just reads off to me."

A shudder ripped through her, and he clasped his hands behind his back to keep from comforting her. "Me, too."

Brooke returned with her jacket on and handed a winter coat to Zoe. "Dusty did call and officially check out this morning. I told Izzy that no one is to go inside that cabin before I take a look. I think we should do that now."

"Agreed," Lincoln said. "Brooke, do you want to drive with Zoe back to the retreat, or would you rather hop in my car?"

"No sense in leaving my car here. Zoe and I will follow behind you."

Cruz hated the relief that flooded through him as he led the way out of the studio and settled back into Lincoln's vehicle. The girls climbed into Brooke's car parked on the street in front of them. He closed his eyes, the sting of Zoe's rejection cutting like a blunt knife against his skin. Now more than ever he needed to nail the bastard stalking her. After last night, he couldn't be with her day after day—night after night—knowing she didn't feel the same way as he did. If he thought he'd suffered from a broken heart when Diana died, that pain was very different then the knowledge the woman he loved didn't want to be with him.

18

Z oe burrowed into the hard chair on the back deck of the lodge, feet tucked under her and a blanket covering her lap. A cup of untouched tea sat beside her on the wide armrest. Too much anxiety boiled in her gut to handle anything—even the weak beverage Brooke fixed her after taking the guys to the cabin Dusty had stayed in.

While Cruz and Lincoln searched Dusty's cabin, she waited with Brooke on the deck at the lodge. The stillness of the frozen lake and the crisp jangle of the light breeze through the pine needles of the evergreens almost made her fool herself into believing today was just another normal day.

Almost.

Just like she could almost make herself believe the reason she wanted to stay back at the lodge was because she didn't want to be reminded of the man who'd stayed at the cabin. That sitting here, tucked away from Cruz wasn't because she couldn't handle being near him. Seeing the hesitation in his eyes when he'd started talking to her about their night together had nearly crushed her. She wasn't a fool. She hadn't thought one night in her arms would make him fall hopelessly in love with her.

It wasn't as if that was the case for her either. She'd been in love with Cruz for years. She just wasn't willing to admit it to anyone. Not even herself. Because, really, what was the point?

"Are you sure you don't want to have a look around the cabin with Lincoln and Cruz?" Brooke asked from her spot beside her.

Watching the frozen lake, Zoe shook her head. "If they find something, they'll tell me and I'll look at whatever it may be. But even if there's something that points to Dusty being the man we're after, I don't want to come face-to-face with the evidence if I don't have to."

Brooke sighed. "Can't say I blame you."

Zoe reached for Brooke's hand and squeezed. Brooke had seen the twisted things a man obsessed would do. She didn't talk about it much, but Zoe knew what Brooke uncovered in the woods behind her cabin last summer still haunted her. Zoe had enough demons. She didn't need to add any more if it could be helped.

The door swung open, and a dark-haired woman Zoe had never seen before stepped outside and lifted her face to the wind. With eyes closed, she sucked in several deep breaths.

"Is everything all right, Mia?" Brooke asked, concern etched at the corners of her mouth.

The woman—Mia—gasped and pressed a palm to her chest. "I'm sorry. I didn't know anyone was out here."

Brooke tapped the empty chair on the other side of her. "No problem. Why don't you take a seat?"

A hesitant smile skittered across Mia's mouth. "Okay. Just for a minute or two." She crossed over the wooden deck and eased into the Adirondack chair. "This view is perfection. I can't wait to see all the trees in bloom."

"Agreed," Zoe said and leaned forward with an extended hand. "Hi, I'm Zoe. It's nice to meet you."

Mia reached over Brooke to take her hand. "Likewise."

Brooke frowned. "You looked upset when you stepped outside."

Sighing, Mia settled against the back of the seat. "I'm not used to such a hostile work environment. Making candy might not be all chocolate rivers and funny looking men, but Meally's Candy was generally a happy place. Here..." She shrugged. "I'm sorry. I don't want to sound ungrateful for this opportunity."

Sympathy flooded Zoe's chest. "Chet's been through a lot lately."

"Everyone's been through a lot." Mia's voice turned whispery and low.

"You're right," Brooke said. "And Chet shouldn't take his pain out on you. You're doing a great job, though. I promise he'll come around."

Mia pressed her lips together. "I don't see that happening any time soon, but he won't drive me away. I need this job."

Something in the fierce way she spoke raised questions for Zoe, but she didn't want to pry into the business of a woman she'd just met. Instead, she focused on something else Mia said. "So you used to work at Meally's? The candy factory in Elm Ridge?"

"The one and only." Mia settled her arms on the wide rests of the chair. "Worked there for three years. I liked it well enough, but I needed something more challenging."

"Oh, you'll find working with Chet challenging all right," Brooke said with a snort.

Mia smiled. "Be careful what you wish for, right?"

Zoe chuckled. She adored Chet, and even understood his sour mood, but he could be intimidating. Especially if Mia didn't understand the reasons for his constant grumpiness. "Do you happen to know a man named Brian? He's an accountant there."

Brooke raised her brows. "Oh yes, the charming Brian from yoga. You ignored me earlier when I brought him up."

Zoe rolled her eyes. "Leo's mom just mentioned he worked there, and I wondered if you knew him. He comes to my yoga class with his nephew a couple times a week."

Frowning, Mia leaned forward. "I've never met him, but I know who he is. Everyone who works at Meally's does."

Mia's forlorn expression caught Zoe off guard.

"What? Not so charming after all?" Brooke asked, her amused eyes on Zoe.

"It's not that." Mia winced. "His wife died last year. Tragic accident. He found her behind their house or something. She'd fallen through the ice in a river."

Zoe glanced at the beautiful lake and a shiver danced down her spine. "How awful. His sister mentioned he'd had a hard time after his wife died, but she hadn't mentioned what happened."

"He stopped coming into work after that."

Zoe furrowed her brow. "How do you know that?"

"He'd always come down to the line and snag free candy." Mia wrinkled her nose. "One of the perks. Mr. Meally even has special wrappers and tins made for employees. A fun little benefit of working there until my waistline grew. The man you're talking about always came down and grabbed tins of candy. Once his wife died, he stopped coming down."

"Sandra said he works from home most of the time. How

awful. To be happy and in love and then one day it's just all ripped away." The blunt edges of grief that never truly went away pushed against her chest. She understood all too well what it was like to have the bottom drop out of her world—the people she loved most lost forever.

Brooke trained her gaze on Zoe like a laser. "Might be a good lesson in living the life you've got while you have the chance."

Zoe twisted her lips. She couldn't imagine losing Cruz in such a tragic way, and she hadn't even told him how she felt. Maybe she should. Brooke might have a point. The time she'd spent with Cruz the last few days made it impossible to deny she was in love with him and after being together, she wasn't sure if she could just go back to the way things were before. If she laid out all of her cards, told Cruz the good the bad and the ugly, what was the worst that could happen?

He could turn away, and she'd lose the friendship that meant so much to her. It was a gamble, and one she didn't have the energy to think about right now. She needed to get through the risk to her life before she could decide if she was ready to risk her heart.

WITH GLOVED HANDS, Cruz flipped open the cabinet doors in the kitchen of Dusty's cabin. A quick glance upon arrival showed Dusty had cleared out all of his things, leaving nothing but rumpled bed sheets behind. "I want to talk to the woman he attacked," Cruz said. "There has to be more to the story."

Lincoln wedged his arm under the couch cushions. "I'll put in another call to the police chief I spoke with, but he wouldn't give me any names before. Wanted to protect the woman's privacy." He straightened and brushed dust from his knees.

"The woman might change her mind if she understands why we need more information on Dusty. The details he provided on the application for the retreat doesn't give us much besides his basic background, and even the sketchy behavior you uncovered does nothing but heighten our suspicion. We need more." He slammed the top cabinet door closed. Nothing but boxed food and cobwebs.

"Careful, man. I know you're frustrated but taking it out on Brooke's property will only piss her off and land me in hot water."

Huffing out an irritated sigh, Cruz plopped onto one of the two kitchen chairs. "Sorry. I'm just in a bad mood."

Crossing his arms over his chest, Lincoln firmed his lips and hooked up an eyebrow. "Something tells me your pissy mood isn't just about not finding a damn thing in this cabin."

"Isn't a possible rapist on the loose enough?" Cruz asked, averting his gaze.

Lincoln snorted. "Don't give me that bullshit. I know you too damn well. Not to mention I saw how you and Zoe acted earlier. Something happened with you two."

There was no use denying it. Lincoln was right, feeding him any kind of lie or half-truth would be a waste of time. But that didn't mean he wanted to discuss what went down with Zoe. "It doesn't matter. Zoe is my friend, and I need to help get her out of this mess by finding the asshole who's after her. Plain and simple."

"There's nothing simple about you and Zoe."

Cruz glared. "Shut up."

Lincoln held up his hands and chuckled. "No offense.

Trust me. I get the whole pretend you're not in love shit. I played that game myself not too long ago. But I was an idiot, and so are you if you don't wake up and do something about your feelings for Zoe."

Swallowing a ball of emotions, Cruz worked his jaw back and forth. He wasn't playing a game. But that didn't mean the two of them were meant to be. "What's between me and Zoe doesn't matter right now. We need to finish searching this place." Rising, he returned to the cabinets and yanked open the door below the sink. Disinfectant and paper towels cluttered around a drain pipe.

"You're right," Lincoln said. "The priority is catching the bad guy. But just remember. You deserve to be happy. You and Diana planned a whole life together, complete with little Sawyer brats to drive you crazy. Even if she's not here, she'd still want that for you. Just like the rest of us do."

Tears threatened to fill Cruz's eyes. What the hell was wrong with him? Must be the fumes from under the sink. It couldn't be the longing in his heart for the life his brother described. Except now, when he closed his eyes, it was Zoe's face he saw beside him.

Just another stupid dream that would never come true.

Lincoln raised his palms. "Okay. I'm done. Let's get this over with." He strolled to the bed and dropped to his knees to look underneath it, then slid a hand under the mattress before standing and moving to the nightstand.

Cruz cleared his throat and pulled out the partially filled trash can. Turmoil brewed inside him. As much as he appreciated Lincoln's good intentions, bringing up Diana and everything he'd lost when she died did nothing to soothe him. Diana *would* want him to be happy, and after five long years, he finally realized that losing her in such a tragic way didn't mean he had to chain himself to a life of misery as punishment for not saving her. But that realization didn't mean a damn thing if the woman he'd fallen for head over heels didn't feel the same way.

Shoving aside the pain gripping his chest, he jostled the knee-high bin and his breath caught. Empty gum wrappers stared up at him. "Peppermint gum wrappers," he called over his shoulders. "It's not much of a clue, but Zoe said her attacker always smells like peppermint. Could be another link to Dusty that we need. Too bad it's not enough to get a couple squad cars to chase after him and bring him back to town."

Lincoln came around the corner, a fierce look blazing his blue eyes. "That might not be enough, but I bet this will." He held out this hand, offering a small scrap of paper. "Found it tucked between the pages of the bible in the top drawer of the nightstand."

"What's this?" Cruz grabbed the thick paper—a polaroid —and turned it around to see the picture. Zoe stood next to a large military tent dressed in fatigues, a gun in her hands and a broad smile on her face. He turned it back around and read the messy blue ink in the corner.

Zoe Peyton. Afghanistan.

Ty's girl.

19

The wind whistled around the corner of the lodge, barreling through the wide deck. Horror latched onto Zoe's throat as she stared down at the picture Cruz had handed her. Her labored breathing made her chest heave. She tore her gaze from the smiling picture of herself—a picture she'd forgotten had ever been taken—and found Cruz's troubled gaze. "I don't understand. This was in Dusty's cabin? In a bible?"

Cruz nodded.

"Why would he have this?" The visible reminder of her past crashed against her, and she closed her eyes, waiting for the surge of panic to lessen.

Brooke took the photo, flipping it over to read the back. "This is from when you were stationed in Afghanistan."

Keeping her eyes latched shut, Zoe nodded. A tear slid down her cheek as memories assaulted her. Memories she worked so damn hard to keep buried.

A strong arm glided over her shoulder, and before she knew what was happening, she was crushed against Cruz's hard chest. She burrowed against him, accepting his

strength and comfort as she threatened to fall apart. Sobs
caught in her throat. She inhaled through her nose, steeling
her nerves and allowing one more moment before pulling
herself together and straightening in her chair. She finally
opened her eyes and stared into the depthless blue of Cruz's
irises. He'd knelt beside her deck chair, crouching low.
"What does this mean?"

"It means we need to figure out Dusty's connection to Ty.
How did he get this picture of you? And why did he lie
about knowing who you were?"

"We asked him if he served with you in Afghanistan,"
Lincoln said, his stance in front of her blocking the midday sun. "He claimed not to know you, even though you
both served in Afghanistan at the same time. We still
looked into it, and you weren't stationed in the same
location."

Cruz rested a palm on her forearm, and the warmth
chased away the terror jangling her nerves. "We should have
looked into other connections. Made sure nothing overlapped. This is big."

"He didn't lie. We didn't serve together. I've never seen
him before, and what were the chances he knew Ty?"

Cruz shrugged. "Slim, but still."

"What now?"

"We have police keeping an eye out for him. His house is
being watched by the local PD, and the highway patrol and
local law enforcement have been given the make and model
of his truck. When we find him, we put an end to this sick
game of his." Cruz rose, and she would have done anything
to grab the neck of his gray t-shirt and pull him back down.
His nearness gave her a strength that instilled a different
kind of fear. A fear of the emptiness his absence would
cause. "Until then, we figure out how Dusty and Ty knew

each other, and why that relationship led Dusty here to you."

She took a deep breath of mountain air. She'd spent so many years keeping her past with Ty shoved into a locked box in the corner of her mind. She may have trusted her friends with her trauma, but the thought of unloading every detail about their relationship sat heavy on her shoulders.

"Are you okay talking about Ty with me around?" Lincoln asked. "I can leave."

His consideration warmed her and made her happy that her friend had found such a thoughtful partner. Not that it surprised her. Lincoln may have a little rougher exterior than Cruz, but the brothers were more alike than not. Kindness was at their core. Waving away his concern, she sank deep in her chair and pulled the warm, red and black checked blanket to her chin. "You already know what happened."

He took a couple steps backward and leaned against the railing. "You want to talk out here or step inside?"

Even though the idea of a warm fire was alluring, she didn't think she could move. Not with so much weighing her down. "Here's fine."

Cruz grabbed the chair on the other side of Brooke and dragged it in front of Zoe. His knees pressed against hers. "What was Ty's last name? I want to run a search on him. Look into his background before he entered the military."

She forced herself to concentrate on just the facts. Only letting her mind work out the information that was necessary to the investigation and nothing more. Nothing traumatizing or painful. Nothing that would break her down all over again if she let it creep into her mind's eye. When she had a moment to herself, to reflect and dig deep into her feelings, then she'd drop her guard and wade through all her emotions. "Ty Buckman."

Cruz glanced over his shoulder at Lincoln, who nodded then grabbed his phone and started working. Refocusing on her, Cruz leaned forward and rested his arms on his thighs. "Do you know anything about his history? Where he was from?"

She blew out a breath and tried to remember anything about the man she'd once fallen for. "He was from Pennsylvania. Oldest of three. Went to college for a year after high school but dropped out to enlist in the Army."

"Any idea where he went to college? Did he have any good friends he talked about from back home?" Cruz asked.

She shrugged. "Nothing comes to mind. At least not off the top of my head. But honestly, we didn't talk much about home. At least not beyond missing a juicy cheeseburger or dreaming about jumping in the creek that ran behind my ma's house. Diving too deep into things back home depressed us."

"Finding out where he went to college should be easy enough," Brooke cut in. "It will show up on a background check."

"Or old social media pages," Lincoln said. He angled his phone screen so Zoe could see it. "Is this him?"

A profile picture of a young man with a shit-eating grin and sparkling green eyes stared up at her and made her skin crawl. Six years had passed since she'd seen his face, but nothing would ever diminish the memory of those eyes. That smile. The face that continued to haunt her dreams. "That's him."

Lincoln swiped at his screen. "Says here he went to Kent State University for a year."

"That's in Ohio, right?" Zoe asked.

Cruz widened his eyes. "That's where Dusty's from."

Zoe swallowed past the lump in her throat as pieces of the puzzle started clicking together. "That might be how Dusty and Ty met but doesn't explain why Dusty would look me up years after Ty's death and come after me."

A buzz sounded, and Cruz stretched back to grab his phone from his pocket. He held up a finger, asking her to wait a second as he answered. "Cruz here." He nodded along to whatever the person on the other line said. "Lincoln and I will be right there." Disconnecting, he put his phone back in his pocket and rose. "A trooper pulled him over on the highway north of Gatlinburg. I'm not sure why he's come after you after all this time, but I will find out."

Zoe squeezed the arms of her chair as anticipation buzzed through her. Finally, the guy they were after was caught. Now it was time to get some answers.

CRUZ WOUND through the unfamiliar halls of the police station where Dusty was detained. The white-washed cinder block walls and smell of stale coffee might be similar to the station in Pine Valley, but that was where the similarities ended. This two-story building on the outskirts of Gatlinburg boasted new computers on all the desks he'd passed and a separate room for interrogating suspects. One that was laughably small compared to the spacious areas throughout the new building.

But he wasn't laughing when he spied Dusty sitting on a hard folding chair in the interrogation room, his hands clenched on top of the white table. His head was down, his gaze fixed on the stain-free beige carpet.

A trooper sat on the chair on the opposite side of the

table. Spotting Cruz and Lincoln in the doorway, he hopped to his feet and extended a hand. "Officer Sawyer?"

Cruz nodded. He hadn't donned his uniform today, but the trooper was expecting him and Lincoln. He shook the man's hand. "Yes. I'm Cruz Sawyer. This is my brother Lincoln."

Lincoln leaned around Cruz and took the trooper's hand. "Nice to meet you. Thanks for bringing this guy in," he said, lifting his chin toward Dusty.

Dusty popped up his head, a deep scowl pressing down his lips. "Why won't you leave me alone?"

The trooper shifted from the shoebox room and squeezed past Cruz to stand in the attached area that looked like the break room. "Nice to meet ya'll. I'm Officer Paulie. Guy hasn't said a damn word until now. Doesn't seem happy, though. I'll leave you fellas alone while you speak with him. Holler when you're done."

"Appreciate it," Cruz said, and waited for him to step into the hallway before taking over the vacated seat. "Wanna bring a chair in here, Linc?"

Lincoln folded his arms over his chest and leaned against the doorjamb. "Don't think there's room. I'll just stand."

Dusty sighed and slumped back against his chair. "What do you want from me? I've answered every question you've asked. I even talked to Zoe and tried to explain myself. Just leave me alone. I only want to go home and forget this whole experience."

"How did you know where Zoe worked?" Cruz jumped right in with both feet. He didn't want to waste time dicking around. He wanted answers, and he wanted them now.

Dusty blinked, long and slow. "She'd mentioned owning a yoga studio in town during one of her classes. There was only one when I looked it up. Thought I'd take a chance she was there when I left town."

"Why?" Lincoln asked. "You said you'd never met her before. You took what, a couple of her classes at the retreat? Why should it matter what she thinks of you?"

Dusty rubbed circles against his temples. "It just does, okay? She's a nice woman, and I don't need her thinking I'm some kind of creep. I've had enough of that."

"Because of the woman you assaulted back in Ohio? I'm sure that attached more than the *creep* label on you." Cruz scratched the back of his neck, fighting every impulse in his body to lunge across the table and plant his fist in the guy's face.

"Seriously?" Dusty shot to his feet.

The quick motion had Cruz reaching for his sidearm.

Dusty shoved his hands in the pockets of his jacket and shook his head, mumbling for a minute before clearing his throat and meeting Cruz's eye. "I told you what happened with that situation. I feel like no matter what I tell you, it's not enough. You've tracked me down twice at that stupid retreat, then you have a trooper pull me over and haul me into a police station to question me again. Tell me what you want from me. What can I say to make you leave me the hell alone?" His voice hitched louder, his face growing red as his attempt to stay calm slipped by the second.

Lincoln dropped his arms to his sides and shifted his weight slightly forward, positioning himself to move quickly if needed.

Cruz fought to remain passive and appear at ease with the mounting tension in the room. He didn't need to escalate Dusty's temper any further. Reaching into his pocket, he pulled out the picture of Zoe from the cabin. Not tearing his gaze from Dusty, he threw the photo on the table. "I want you to tell me why you lied about knowing who Zoe was, and why you had this picture hidden in your room. I want you to tell me how you know Ty Buckman."

All the color drained from Dusty's face, making the light brown whiskers on his chin stand out in stark contrast to his pale cheeks. His jaw dropped. He pulled his hand from his pocket and wiped the shocked expression from his open mouth.

The sudden motion caused something to fall from his pocket and land on the floor. Cruz leaned over the table to get a better look. A set of keys laid at his feet. An odd-looking eagle head was attached to the metal keyring, frayed braids of blue and gold plastic flowing from it.

The world went still. The man who'd broken into Zoe's studio didn't have strands of hair attached to his keys, it was an old, piece of shit lanyard.

Cruz's head whipped up to eye the man who was responsible for all of this. And that man was standing right in front of him.

20

Zoe tapped the tip of her finger against the end table beside her. She sat on the worn sofa with her legs crossed, her dangling foot shaking from its spot above the soft rug. Some nature program hummed along on the television, but she couldn't focus on it. Nervous energy zipped through her body, needing to be released.

She could grab a mat and try to quiet her mind, but it'd be a waste of time. No way she'd squelch her anxiety until Cruz and Lincoln returned and told her Dusty was behind bars—until they confirmed he was the man who'd attacked her. Until they'd given her the reasons why.

Sucking in a shaky breath, Zoe jumped to her feet and crossed the room to the lone window. She peeled back the curtain and stared into the parking lot. The sun shined bright against a blue sky, hiding the cold that had refused to leave the last few days. She could go for a run, but not alone, and Brooke was busy in the kitchen, playing referee to Mia and Chet's constant bickering as they prepared lunch.

Besides, she didn't want anyone's company right now. Making small talk or answering any more questions sounded like torture. But sitting alone in this empty room, with only her thoughts to keep her company, was just as horrible. Maybe stepping outside and changing her scenery would help. She could stop by the kennel where the therapy dogs were housed and grab Wyatt. He'd be better company than anyone else.

Decision made, she swiped her phone from the coffee table and shrugged into her coat before darting through the door. She kept her head bent against the harsh wind. She hurried down the wide steps of the wraparound porch and onto the sidewalk that led to the path toward the kennel just as a silver SUV raced into the parking lot.

Halting, she watched the unfamiliar vehicle speed toward her, screeching to a stop with the passenger side window facing her. The window slid down, and Brian's frantic face appeared.

Confusion had her dipping her brows low. "Brian? What are you doing here?"

"Have you seen Leo? Talked to him at all?" He hurled the question at her, eyes wide and full of alarm.

She took a step forward, closing the gap between her and the car. "Not since this morning. At the Mommy and Me class."

He tightened his grip on the steering wheel and squeezed his eyes shut for a beat. "Damnit. Where could he be? Why would he run off like that?"

A fist squeezed her heart. Gone was the fear for her own well-being, replaced by a bone-chilling horror. "What do you mean? Leo ran away?"

Brian shoved a hand through his hair, gripping the light strands and pulling slightly. "Sandra called me about an hour ago. She's scared out of her mind. He was in his room, and she thought he was taking a nap. But when she went to check on him, the window was open and he was gone."

She covered her mouth with her trembling fingers. "Did she call the police?"

"Yes. She's a wreck. I need to help. Need to find him. I shouldn't have cancelled on him today. It always messes with him, and he's been so out of sorts lately." He rested his forehead against the wheel, emotion pitching in his hysteric voice. "I thought maybe he'd tried to get to you. He loves being around you."

Chances of Leo attempting to make it up the mountain to the retreat were low. Biting into her bottom lip, she tried to think of where Leo would go that his mom or uncle wouldn't have already looked. "What about the yoga studio? It's closed, but he might have gone there. Or maybe next door to Crawley's Confections. He loves those doughnuts."

Brian straightened, a flash of hope widening his eyes. "I drove by the studio but didn't think about the bakery. Sandra is home. The police told her to stay there in case Leo comes back. Can you come with me? Maybe we can think of other places in town he might have run to?"

Hesitation had her glancing over her shoulder to the lodge. She should let Brooke know if she planned to leave. Her friend would be upset if Zoe just vanished, and she had no clue where she'd gone.

"Please." Brian's voice cracked and a tear slid over his cheek. "I'm freaking out. I can't lose that little boy. Can't go through that kind of loss again."

Her heart lurched. She still didn't have her own car to just follow Brian and running inside for someone else's keys would waste precious time. She'd grabbed her phone before leaving. She could make a call if she felt unsafe, but if something happened to Leo that she could have helped prevent, she'd never forgive herself.

Opening the passenger side door, she jumped inside. Her feet brushed against debris under the dashboard. Warm air blew from the vents, but her teeth chattered. No way she could let Brian search for his missing nephew alone. Not after everything he'd already lost. "Of course I'll help you," she said, forcing a tight smile. "Leo will be fine. I'm sure we'll find him sitting at a table with Mrs. Crawley, eating a glazed doughnut." She swung the door to close it, but something got caught and caused the door to stay ajar. She shifted her foot, and something fell from the floor into the gravel of the parking lot.

"I can't thank you enough," Brian said, taking off before she latched the door.

Leaning to the side, she grabbed the handle and pulled until the door shut. She'd pick up whatever she'd dropped when she got back. "You don't need to do this alone. I'm glad to come along."

She needed to text Brooke and let her know what was going on. Then call Cruz. He might be with Dusty, but he could have more information about Leo he could share with her. But first, she had to hook her seatbelt. Reaching across her chest, her eye caught on the mess at her feet. Crumpled papers and metal tins of some kind.

Curiosity piqued, she leaned forward. The tins had a red and white label, and bold black letters spelled out Meally's. Below that, the type of candy found inside.

Peppermints.

Her stomach rolled, and she fought to keep her composure as Brian took a turn down the mountain. So what? Mia had told her Brian often took tins of candy from work, and he'd been there this morning. It made sense that he grabbed some while he was there, and peppermints were a common enough candy.

Refusing to turn her head, she slid her gaze to the side and the world tilted on its axis. Brian's keys dangled from the ignition, what looked like strands of auburn hair flowing from the keyring.

Her breath caught in her throat, and she tried to be as inconspicuous as possible as she reached for her phone in her coat pocket. She pulled the device out just enough for her fingers to tap against the screen.

Brain flicked a glance in her direction. He dropped his eyes to her side then back up to meet her gaze. "What are you doing?"

She swallowed, forcing a breath past the lump in her throat. "Nothing. Just thinking where Leo could be. I hope he's not outside. It's so cold."

Without warning, Brian grabbed her phone from her hand. "You're not going to need this."

It took every ounce of control not to react, not to let her face betray her feelings. "What are doing? I was going to call Cruz and ask about Leo. Maybe they've already found him."

She reached for the phone, and Brian jerked the wheel to send her back to her side of the car. He righted the vehicle again, then placed her phone in his jeans pocket. "I don't think so. You don't need Cruz. Not now. Not ever. You're mine, and there's nothing anyone can do to take you from me."

"WHAT THE HELL IS THAT?" Cruz roared, veering around the table to scoop Dusty's keys off the ground. His sudden movement caused Dusty to stagger backward, bracing his hands on the wall to keep his balance.

Frowning, Lincoln took a step forward. "What the—?"

Cruz pressed into Dusty's personal space. He thrust the keys in the air, causing the metal to clink together. "You sonofabitch. I *knew* it was you."

"What are you talking about?" Dusty's eyes widened to the size of saucers.

Cruz wiggled the tattered lanyard. "You've had us chasing our tails this whole time, except for one little clue. Your stupid keychain was caught on the bakery's security footage. It was hard to make out what it was, but not too many things can look like a freaking tassel."

Dusty held up his hands and shook his head. "That's a lanyard I bought from college. It doesn't mean a damn thing. And what bakery? I don't know what in God's name you're talking about."

Lincoln rested a hand on Cruz's shoulder, and he shrugged it off. He didn't want his brother hovering over him, keeping him calm. Telling him to have a cool head. They'd just caught the bastard who'd tried to rape Zoe. Who'd almost killed his best friend in the whole damn world. "Enough lies. Why come after Zoe? Tell me about all the other women."

Tears clouded Dusty's eyes, and he pressed his lips together. His nostrils flared as he breathed in and out through his nose. "For the last time. I don't know what you're talking about."

"Let's just settle down a second," Lincoln said, lowering his outstretched palms through the air as if to make them all sit. "Go back to Ty Buckman and the picture you brought with you to the retreat."

Red crept over Dusty's cheeks, and he dropped his gaze.

"Ty and I were roommates our freshmen year of college. We stayed in touch after we enlisted. He told me about this girl. Zoe. I wanted to meet her."

"That was six years ago," Cruz said through clenched teeth. His patience was slipping, but he needed to watch what he said. He didn't want to give away more of Zoe's story than Dusty already knew. "Why come looking for her now? And why not tell her you knew her ex?"

"After he died...well, let's just say his death hit me hard. Call it survivor's guilt or PTSD. Whatever the reason, I lost myself for a little bit. I turned to alcohol, drugs...anything to numb the pain." On a sigh, Dusty finally lifted his head and met Cruz's glare head on. "One day, when I hit rock bottom, I went to an AA meeting. I found myself, and in the process, realized I needed to right my wrongs."

"What does Zoe have to do with your wrongs?" Cruz said, not knowing if he should believe the guy's bullshit or not. So far, Dusty hadn't proven himself trustworthy. Also the mangled plastic keychain in his hand proved more than enough evidence in Cruz's mind that Dusty was guilty.

"I know what Ty did to her," Dusty said, flinching. "The guy was my buddy, but he had a dark side. It got worse when he went overseas. He told me what happened with Zoe, and it made me sick. Knowing he died before he could find a way to make amends to her—knowing she never got justice —ate me up inside."

"What about the girl from the bar?" Lincoln asked. Disgust dripped from every word. "Wouldn't your buddy's sins make you want to act differently? Not do the same shit he'd pulled?"

Dusty scrubbed a palm over his face. "That happened before I got sober. My drinking isn't an excuse, but I tried to make things right—find a way to fix it—but nothing's worked and I have to live with that. I don't remember hurting her, don't remember not backing away when she told me to, but I won't say it didn't happen. Won't make her look like she wasn't telling the truth if there's the tiniest possibility that she is."

Cruz's mind spun. Dusty's words rang true, but there was no way to know for sure. Not to mention he had no alibis for any of the times Zoe was attacked. But what about for the night when someone broke into Lexi's bookstore? Grabbing his phone, he pulled up the information he needed on Lexi's case and located the date of her attack. "Can you account for your whereabouts a year ago January 23?"

"What?"

"Just answer the question," Lincoln said.

Dusty blew out a shaky breath and closed his eyes, as if trying to pull the date into his memory bank. "Last winter I was still pretty new to my job. I would have worked the night shift until after February." He opened his eyes and looked from Lincoln to Cruz. "Why?"

"Because if you have an alibi for that night, we know you aren't the guy we're looking for." Irritation clawed at Cruz's chest. Dusty checked all the boxes of who they were after. Not only did he have the means, but possible motive with his connection to Ty. A reason for wanting to punish Zoe he hadn't yet revealed. Cruz wanted the bad guy to be Dusty, because if Dusty wasn't their guy, then who was?

Cruz's phone vibrated in his hand, and Brooke's name and picture flashed on his screen. He accepted the call then pressed the phone to his ear. "Hey, Brooke. What's up?"

"Have you heard from Zoe?" she asked.

The urgency in her voice made alarm bells blast in his brain. "No. Isn't she with you at the lodge?"

"She's not here, and I don't know where she went. I tried

her phone, but she won't answer. Won't text me back. She's not in her room and none of the staff have seen her. She's gone, Cruz."

Dread curdled in his stomach, and the realization of what happened almost knocked him to his knees. He'd left Zoe's side, left her with the promise of capturing the person who was after her. In reality, he'd left her vulnerable, confident that her attacker was no longer a threat. Dusty wouldn't tell them he'd worked the night in question if he couldn't prove it. Cruz would verify his claim, and if Dusty was telling the truth, he was innocent.

All the air left Cruz's lungs, and he dropped his hand to his side as his gaze sought Lincoln's. "We need to get back to Pine Valley. Zoe's missing."

21

Zoe's paralyzing fear played weird tricks with the passage of time. Unlike the traumatic experiences of her past where the world seemed to stop spinning, making the excruciating moments last a lifetime, time whizzed ahead now. The trees outside the SUV window whirred by. She'd jumped into Brian's vehicle shortly before lunchtime, and the blinking numbers that never changed on the dashboard did nothing to clue her in to how long she'd been trapped in the speeding car.

The scenery was both familiar and foreign. The white-tipped trees and surrounding mountain range could be the same picture in multiple spots in the area. No unique landscape marked the way through the generic backdrop. Dark clouds swept into the sky, the threat of more snow heavy in the air. Nerves tightened in her stomach. Slick roads in a speeding car were the last things she needed to worry about right now.

Brian had cranked the radio, blasting heavy metal until the bass threatened to burst through the speakers. He didn't say a word. He drove with a singular focus that was unsettling—down country roads and around hairpin turns. Memories of her car crash had her tensing her muscles and bracing for impact as Brian continued toward his destination.

Licking her lips, she replayed her options. Not like she had many. The only thing she'd come up with was waiting for the car to slow and throwing herself from a moving vehicle. The idea wasn't appealing, but it was better than whatever Brian had planned. He'd eluded the police for close to a year, keeping his identity concealed from them as well as the women he'd stalked and attacked. There was no telling what he would do now that his cover was blown. Something told her he wouldn't just let her walk away.

A curve in the road appeared, and Zoe held onto the handle, anticipating the slower speed it would take for Brian to keep the car safely in its lane. This may be her only chance for escape. Adrenaline zipped through her veins and pounded in her ears. She could do this. She could make the leap and run through the trees until she found safety.

The car slowed, and Brian turned the radio down, as if he could sense the plan in her mind and wanted to hear it better. He cast her a quick glance, and she stilled. Not wanting to show her hand. "We're almost there," he said. "Leo will be so happy to see you."

His statement slammed against her, stealing both her breath and her plan. "What do you mean?"

Sliding a hand from the wheel, he clapped his palm against her knee and squeezed. "Leo. He's waiting for us. I told him he better be good and stay where I put him, or you'd be very disappointed. He's so excited you're part of our family now."

Bile slid up her throat. If Leo was in danger, she couldn't jump out of the car and run. Brian was dangerous, and just because Leo was his nephew, it didn't mean he wouldn't hurt him.

"Is he at your house?" She scanned the roadside, searching for any signs to clue her in to where exactly she was. She remembered Leo mentioning that Brian didn't live in Pine Valley. But if he worked in Elm Ridge, his house couldn't be too far away.

A thin strip of gravel shot off the road right before the curve, and Brian bounced the SUV onto the lane. "You ask too many questions. Don't worry. We'll be there soon."

Sweat coated her palms. She studied the area, searching for an escape route. Once she figured out how to secure Leo, she'd have to make a run for it. Maybe there was a trail nearby that would lead them to safety. The vehicle jostled along the uneven terrain, and she tightened her grip on the doorhandle. No way this was a driveway that led to a home. Upturned roots broke through packed dirt and bare branches pummeled the sides of the SUV.

A small clearing appeared with a wooden structure in the middle. Bigger than the hunting blinds that were scattered along the mountains, but not by much. A square stoop led to a dark brown door—the same color as the bark of the logs that made up the hut. A metal chimney stuck out of the top of one corner, smoke billowing into the air.

Brian parked at the end of the lane and flashed a wide grin. "We're here. I've waited so long. I never thought I'd get the chance to bring you here. This is so much better than I'd expected. The waiting. The planning. It's all added to the sweet anticipation." He clapped his hands together. "Let's head inside. Leo really shouldn't be alone this long." He leaned forward and pressed a kiss against her cheek. "Now, don't do anything stupid. I'd hate to punish our Leo because you made a bad decision." He jumped out then rounded the hood to open her door.

Not wanting him to touch her, she hurried out and walked in front of him to the structure. She darted her gaze around the isolated land and noted a trail. Running wasn't an option right now—not with Leo inside—but if she could grab the boy and get out, the trail might lead to help.

Nausea swam in her stomach as she opened the door, stepping inside and scanning the open concept that squeezed in a kitchen and living room. A door at the back of the space either led to a bathroom or outside.

"What do you think?"

She spun around to Brian, standing with his arms spread wide.

"It's not fancy, but it's my own little slice of heaven." Brian peeled off his coat then tossed it onto the back of one of the two kitchen chairs. "*Our* little slice of heaven."

Zoe strained her ears, listening for any signs of Leo. "Where's Leo?"

A deep laugh bellowed from Brian. "You didn't really think I'd kidnap my own nephew, did you? Nah. I need him safe and happy. He's my little wing man."

Pressing her hands to her stomach, she took a step in retreat. "Your what?"

"My wing man," Brian said, shrugging in such a casual way it made her skin crawl. "Couldn't get into Mommy and Me class without a kid, could I?"

Reality buckled her knees. Brian used his nephew to find the women he'd attack. Earn their trust. Learn their routines. Sandra had mentioned Brian taking Leo on outings. He wasn't spending time with Leo to make him feel loved, he was using the little boy to trick his prey into letting down their guards.

CRUZ CATAPULTED up the porch steps at the lodge and stormed inside the lobby, Lincoln close behind. Brooke, Chet, and the new kitchen assistant rushed forward. "Have you heard from Zoe?" he asked, although he already knew the answer. If Zoe had contacted Brooke, Brooke would have called right away to let him know.

"No. I contacted the police." Brooke leaned against Lincoln and rubbed her hands up and down her arms. "A few officers came by. I told them what I knew. They watched the security footage of the front parking lot. Zoe came outside and was approached by a silver SUV. She got inside without a fight. That was a little over an hour ago. No sign of her or the vehicle since."

Lincoln held Brooke close. "We spoke with the chief. He filled us in on what they were doing to find her."

"What about Dusty?" Brooke asked. "Was that a dead end?"

Cruz left Lincoln to explain what they'd learned and ran to the room he'd shared with Zoe. He trusted his fellow officers to do their job, and do it well, but they didn't know Zoe like he did. Wouldn't understand any little hints or clues she may have left. He burst inside and the quietness of the space sent his heart to his throat. He took a moment as pain pressed against his chest before he snapped into cop-mode. Standing around with misty eyes, letting his mind wander to worst case scenarios wouldn't do Zoe any good. He needed to do what he was trained for—look at the facts, find the clues, and find Zoe.

He worked his way around the room, getting halfway through before the rest of the gang joined him in his search. Longing gripped him when he got to the bed, the sheets still rumpled from his night with Zoe. He swallowed hard and looked away.

"I don't see anything in here that helps us," Brooke said.

He turned away from the spot where he'd laid with Zoe and fisted his hands in his hair. He had to approach this logically. "Where would she go? She wouldn't have left without telling someone. And she wouldn't take off with someone she didn't trust completely."

Lincoln shook his head. "I don't know, man. Nothing in here is telling us anything."

"Then let's look outside." Cruz led the way back outside and stood in the same spot Zoe would have been when approached by whoever was in the SUV. A few snowflakes drifted down from heavy, gray clouds. He crouched low and studied the tracks. Nothing distinguishable, but he followed them toward the front of the parking lot.

Something caught his eye among a cluster of rocks. He kicked away the stones and uncovered the bottom of a metal tin. Using the tip of his index finger, he flipped it over and let out a growl of frustration. "An empty tin of peppermints," he called over his shoulder. "Doesn't tell me a damn thing. Anyone can buy these stupid things from Meally's. Hell, I always keep some in my truck." He squinted at the label, something not sitting quite right. "The label looks different, though." He wasn't sure if that meant something, but his instincts screamed it was a clue.

"Did you say Meally's?" Mia approached him with caution in her dark eyes. "I used to work there. Different tins are used for employees. Mr. Meally thought it was a fun perk." Frowning, she leaned forward. "This is one of the employee tins."

"Like the one Brian always grabbed?" Brooke asked.

Cruz spun to pin her with a stare. "Brian? Like that kid's

uncle who takes Zoe's yoga class?" He hadn't liked the guy when they'd met, but he didn't like any man who flirted with Zoe.

"We talked about it just this morning," Brooke said. "The kid, Leo, was at class this morning with his mom. The mom said Brian had to go into work. We realized Mia and Brian worked at the same place when it was brought up."

Adrenaline spiked Cruz's blood pressure. Damnit. "Zoe would trust him, but would she have just hopped in the car and taken off like that?"

Brooke pressed a palm against her chest, rubbing the spot just above her heart. "Not unless she felt like she didn't have any other choice."

Lincoln scowled. "What could this guy have possibly said to make her act so quick? Take that kind of risk?"

A memory of Zoe's smile when she'd hugged Leo flashed in his mind, and everything clicked. "The sonofabitch used the kid. We need to call the mother and make sure Leo is okay. Then we need to find out everything we can about Brian. He has to have Zoe."

Cruz would bet his life on it and do whatever it took to get her back. And when he did, he'd forget all the bullshit he'd believed for so damn long. He'd pull her into his arms, kiss the hell out of her, and tell her how much he loved her. Because once he had her, there was no way he would ever let her go again.

22

D isappointment had Cruz shoving his phone back in his pocket as he stood on the front porch of Sandra Livingston's townhouse, waiting for her to answer the door. He'd called his boss and filled him in on what he'd learned about Brian. His gut instinct and the few facts he'd uncovered weren't enough to secure a warrant to search the guy's house, but officers had been sent to his residence.

"No one was home," he told Brooke.

Lincoln was back at the station, doing all he could to find more information about Brian, but Brooke thought Sandra might be more comfortable speaking with Cruz if she was present. Not only was she a woman, but she'd met Sandra that morning. Knowing what an asset Brooke was, Cruz had accepted her offer.

Brooke rested a hand on his arm. "We'll find Zoe."

Cruz nodded. Just because Brian's house was empty, that didn't mean Cruz was wrong. He just needed to figure out where Brian would take Zoe. He'd contacted Tasha, who'd met him at Serenity Mountain Studio and retrieved the contact information for Sandra. He'd called, giving Leo's mom a heads up that he was on his way.

The door opened and a medium-sized woman with eyes the same deep brown as her son's greeted Cruz with a frown. "Hello?" Her weary gaze landed on Brooke, and she opened the door a little wider before glancing over her shoulder. "Leo's in the kitchen," she said, facing Cruz. "I don't want him to hear this conversation. You can step inside, but I'd like to stand here to talk. Not like there's much for me to say."

The defensive set of her shoulders and harsh tone told Cruz that Sandra wouldn't be a wealth of knowledge.

Brooke entered the home first, offering a small smile. "I know this has to seem like a lot, but it's really important we talk to you about Brian."

"There's nothing to tell," she said on a hiss of breath. "My brother's been through a lot the past year, and the last thing he needs is a bunch of cops poking around his business again."

"Again?" Cruz asked, shutting the door behind him. His feet sank into soft carpet that stretched the length of the rectangular living room. Framed photos hung on the cream-colored walls and worn furniture cluttered around an old tube television. An L-shaped counter separated the living room from the kitchen. The back of Leo's head was visible at the table, headphones over his ears.

"When his wife died, he was questioned. They just needed to make sure the drowning was accidental."

Chills danced down Cruz's spine. "And they were sure it was?"

"Yes," Sandra snapped. "She stepped onto the ice and fell through. Brian was a wreck. He loved Megan more than anything."

Questioning spouses in a suspicious death wasn't unusual, but something must have raised a red flag for the police to hesitate to deem the death accidental. He'd send Lincoln a text, telling him to ask for the report and see if anything stuck out. "I'm sure losing his wife was difficult, but I need to ask. Did they have a good relationship?"

Sandra's lips twitched and silence hung in the air.

"Please, Sandra," Brooke pressed.

Sandra sighed. "They fought sometimes, but what couple doesn't? And Megan...she was dramatic, okay? I hate speaking ill of the dead, especially a sister-in-law I loved, but she wasn't an easy woman. That doesn't mean Brian did anything. He'd never hurt her."

Cruz tightened his jaw, putting together all the facts he'd gathered. The attacks in the area started around a year ago. Right around the time Brian's wife died. Could there be a connection with the woman Brian was married to and the women he targeted after her death? "Do you have a picture of Megan?"

"Why?" Sandra asked, frowning.

"It might prove helpful," Brooke said. "We never know what the one thing might be we need in a situation like this."

"What you need is to leave my brother alone. He's a good man." Sandra huffed but pointed toward the wall to her side. "Here's one from their wedding."

Cruz stepped around her and studied the photo. Brian all smiles in a black tuxedo. His wife—Megan—with auburn hair flowing in loose curls down her back and big green eyes. "She looks like Zoe and Lexi."

"Who's Lexi?" Sandra asked.

Leo popped around the corner with a tablet pressed to his belly. "She's the bookstore lady."

Cruz stilled, his heart pounding in his tight chest, then lowered himself to Leo's eye level. "The bookstore lady?"

Leo cocked his head to the side. "You're the policeman I saw at my yoga class."

"Yes, I am. Can you tell me about Lexi? How do you know her?"

"She tells the best stories. My uncle used to take me to story hour there. It was kind of far, but that made it even more special. But then he said we had to stop. My uncle likes to take me to special places."

His gut knotted, but he had to keep asking questions. "What other special places does he take you?"

Leo swished his lips from side to side. "Well, he found the yoga place where Zoe works. I love going there. And movie theaters and this park with a stage where they had plays. I was sad when we stopped going. He told me we couldn't go see Zoe anymore. I don't want to stop seeing Ms. Zoe, though. She's my favorite. I told Uncle Brian that, but he got mad."

Cruz's mouth went dry. Holy hell. Brian used his nephew as bait—walking, talking, loveable bait. "Why did you stop going to all these places?"

Leo shrugged. "I dunno."

Cruz made a mental note to search the professions of all the women who'd reported a rape or burglary in the last year.

Sandra pulled Leo to her and put her hands on his shoulders. "What is this about?" Concern clouded over her earlier irritation, as if she was catching on that something was happening. Something bad. Something involving her son.

"Lexi is a woman we spoke with who'd been assaulted. Another woman who resembles both Megan and Zoe." Cruz stood and winced, not wanting to upset the boy but needing to be frank with Sandra so she'd finally understand he needed her help. "Do you have any idea where Brian could be right now? Is there a special place he takes Leo when the two of them aren't searching for activities?" The word soured on his tongue. Brian hadn't searched for fun events to share with his nephew. He was trolling for his next victim, using an innocent child to earn women's trust.

"We always go fun places," Leo said, his wide grin breaking Cruz's heart in two. "He said we can go to the park when the cold goes away. Until then, he'll just enjoy his slice of heaven and watch the snow."

"Slice of heaven?" Brooke asked. "Have you ever been there, Leo?"

Leo shook his head. "Nah. Uncle Brian says it's a special place. A place where his dreams always come true." He giggled. "He's so silly."

"Oh my God. I know where he is." A paleness swept over Sandra's features, leaving her looking frail. "Our dad had a little cabin, if you can even call it that, in the woods. Brian loves to fish in the summer. There's a small river that runs behind the cabin. The same river where Megan drowned."

"Can you tell me where it is?" Cruz grabbed his phone and called Lincoln. He'd need backup. Not like he'd wait for it to storm the gates and find the asshole who'd taken Zoe. He just prayed he got to her before it was too late.

Hot, raw anger ebbed through Zoe. Hadn't Brian used Leo enough? Now, he was lying about kidnapping the boy to keep her in check, and she'd fallen for it? Just like she'd fallen for Ty all those years ago. But no more. She wouldn't fall for any more bullshit. Brian stood between her and the door she'd just walked through, leaving her only one option. The door to the left of the kitchen.

She took off in a flash, bolting for the door. She yanked it open, and defeat threatened to stall her when she spied a twin bed with a thick, brown sleeping bag on top of it shoved against the wall. A bedroom. She turned to shut the door.

Brian growled and leapt forward.

She slammed the door shut and turned the lock on the brass knob. Revulsion danced down her throat. She couldn't stop and think about what Brian planned to do in this room —in that bed—or she'd crumple.

"Open the door." Brian banged a fist against the flimsy wood, and the barrier jumped on the hinges with each thud.

The door wouldn't stay in place long. All it would take was one good kick to break it off the wall. She ran to the uncovered window, unlatched the rusty locks, and tried to lift the glass, but it didn't budge. Old, cracked paint lined the bottom of the window, keeping it sealed shut. Zoe reached into the pocket of her coat and pulled out the keys Brooke had given her to her room and the lodge. She shoved the edge of the metal into the crack under the window, using all her strength to loosen the paint. The key slid through, and she put the keyring back in her pocket and tried again to lift the window. The house groaned with the effort, the old wood creaking.

"Damnit, Zoe. I'm not playing around. Open. The. Door." A heavy *thunk* accentuated the last three words, the hinges groaning in protest against the force of Brian's weight.

Zoe gritted her teeth as she moved the glass up inch by inch. Whistles of wind slithered through the growing crack, and she pushed harder. Ignoring her burning biceps until the window was high enough for her to shimmy herself through. Bracing her hands on the windowsill, she pulled herself over then hopped down onto the frozen grass.

The door slammed open, and Brian stormed into the bedroom.

She burst toward the woods. She didn't have a phone and had no idea where she was. Her only chance was outrunning Brian and finding help. Hopefully Brian's endurance was as poor as his yoga skills. Taking off in a sprint, she headed toward the trail she'd spied on the way in. Snowflakes fluttered down from the sky, each flake stinging her wind burnt face like shrapnel. Keeping her feet on the narrow path, she darted into a patch of trees. Branches slapped at her face. She raised her arms to shield herself, but she kept moving. Kept running as fast as she could. Fallen logs littered the snow-covered ground. She struggled to keep on her feet as she leapt over them. The eerie cull of vultures circled overhead, mere shadows under the canopy of trees that blocked out the sun.

The sound of moving brush and stomping feet from behind filled her lungs with fear, making it even harder to breathe. She fought the desire to look around and search for Brian. Any movement that wasn't forward was a waste of time and could be the difference between escape and torture.

"You have nowhere to go, Zoe," Brian called. "I know these woods. You don't. And there's nothing around for miles. Be a good girl and come back to the house. We'll have a good time. I promise." His vow echoed through the woods.

Her stomach twisted. A good time? Brian was a sick bastard. Nothing about what he planned to do would be a good time. She pushed herself faster, willing her mind to ignore her quivering limbs. The cold air burned her throat. She searched for anything she could use. Anything that could help her. Nothing was around but trees and underbrush and dirt. Moisture seeped into her tennis shoes, making her feet turn to ice.

A twig snapped to her side. Close. Too close. Brian was gaining ground. Zoe ventured off the path. Maybe if she could hide, he'd pass her and she could circle back to the shack. Find a phone and get the hell out of here. She ducked and weaved between evergreens, staying low and hiding between the coverage of pointy needles.

The snowflakes became fatter, falling in front of her face in a heavy sheet, obscuring her view. The cold air was still and quiet. Zoe paused, listening and waiting. She pressed her back against the rough bark of an ancient oak tree, her breaths heaving in and out. Cramps tightened her calf muscles and her lungs burned. A squirrel skittered across the path, the movement making her heart jump.

A hand latched onto her wrist from the other side of the tree. "I told you it was no use running."

A scream caught in her throat, and she twisted her arm and jerked down, releasing herself from Brian's grip. She lunged away from him. Thick snowflakes fell in her eyes. She slipped on the wet ground, sliding on a steep incline and trying not to faceplant on her way down the treeless hill. She shot out her arms for balance, steadying herself once she found flat ground. Zoe stumbled forward, her feet gliding on something smooth and slick. She glanced down and her heart leapt into her throat.

Brian rounded the tree and grinned. "Look what you did now. Landed on a frozen river. Too bad the ice is so thin in some spots, and there's no telling where it might break. Poor Megan took that risk once and went right through. She thought she'd get away from me. She was wrong."

Zoe didn't have time to think about that startling confession and what it meant for Brian's poor, dead wife. She needed a plan. Brian stood with his legs planted wide, ready to pounce in any direction she chose to climb back up the incline. Even if she attempted to move left or right along the frozen edge, Brian had the upper hand. Turning, she gauged the distance to the far bank of the river. A good ten feet laid between her and the other side. Not that far, but if Brian was right, the thin ice at the center of the river could break under her weight.

Knowing she didn't have a choice, she put one foot slowly in front of the other. *Please, God. Don't let the ice break.* Adrenaline made her teeth chatter. She kept her arms out to her sides for balance. Swirls of white and blue blended together and crystallized on the frozen water. The ice would be beautiful if she wasn't currently trying to traverse its deadly sparkle.

Zoe was halfway to the other side and excitement beat a steady rhythm in her chest. A quick glance behind her showed Brian taking a tentative step on the ice.

Damn. The frozen water might hold her weight but add a two-hundred-and-something pound man, and it was a different story. Refocusing on her goal, she held her breath and took another step toward the opposite side of the river.

A sharp crack halted her movement. She stilled, waiting. Terror stole her breath. Being trapped under there was a fate worse than death. The ice splintered. Her breath hitched in her throat, and she ran for the safety of the solid ground. The ice shifted, knocking her off balance. "Help!" she yelled, as she struggled to stay upright. Struggled to keep moving toward safety six feet away—close enough to see the scatter of snowflakes on the edge of the opposite bank but too far to reach even if she jumped as far as she could. Water rushed to the surface, creating a large chasm that swallowed Zoe. Cold water engulfed her. She closed her eyes as pain erupted inside her body, the frigid temperatures more than she could bear. She opened her eyes and panic clawed at her chest. White ice encased her, keeping her trapped below. The swift water pulled her downstream. She held her breath and skimmed her fingertips against the barrier holding her prisoner. She needed to find an opening in the ice. Needed air. Needed out of this icy coffin sucking her down to the unknown.

23

Tires slid against slick asphalt as Cruz pulled onto the lane Sandra had described. Without her cooperation, it would have taken ages to find the property still listed under Sandra's father's name. The sprawling acreage would have come up in a search, but the off-the-beaten-path clearing where the tiny cabin was located would have taken hours to locate.

Brooke bounced in her seat beside him. "There's the SUV." She pointed out the window, as if he couldn't see for himself.

But he understood her excitement. Zoe was here. He just hoped he'd made it in time before anything happened to her. He'd never forgive himself if he was too late. Too slow to put the pieces together. Too slow to act. Just like before—playing out like a sick and twisted *Groundhog Day*. His chest tightened, and he had to remind himself to keep breathing. Keep moving.

Parking beside the other vehicle, he shut off the engine and shot a quick text to Lincoln with their coordinates. "Lincoln's on the way with backup. I want him to know exactly where we are."

"In the meantime, you've got me." Brooke reached behind her back for her gun and checked the safety. "My knee might be shot, but my aim is golden."

Securing his own weapon, he nodded and hurried out of the car. With his gun trained in front of him, he swept over the SUV, making sure it was empty before jogging to the front stoop. He stayed low, Brooke at his heels, and blinked to keep the fat flakes of snow from getting in his eyes. Footprints dented the light dusting of powder that led to the door. Two sets.

Brian and Zoe.

Anger pulsed inside Cruz, and he bit the inside of his cheek to keep himself in check. He needed a clear head right now. Steeling his nerves, he turned the knob and swung open the door. He whipped inside to find an empty room.

Cruz crossed the living room/kitchen combo and swept into a bedroom. A single bed. A duffle bag in the corner. No sign of Zoe.

A gust of wind blew in through an open window, and he peered outside to find a cluster of footprints. "She went out the window." Hope blossomed in his chest. Brian might have brought Zoe here, but she'd used her wits and escaped, at least briefly.

Brooke fled back to the front, and he followed. Once outside, he took the lead and rounded the house to the prints in the back. "Should be fairly easy to find them," he said. The snow might make visibility more difficult, but a trail would lead them right to Zoe.

"Brian would have done the same thing." Brooke shuddered. "Followed Zoe's footprints."

He tightened his grip on the gun, unwilling to believe Brian got her.

An ear-splitting scream pierced the quiet, afternoon sky.

"Zoe!" Cruz took off down a narrow path that led to the woods, leaving Brooke to follow behind him. Outstretched limbs scratched his cheeks. His booted feet pounded through the forest as he scanned every inch he passed. Another scream had him veering off a narrow trail, dodging between thick tree trunks and hopping over upturned roots. The uneven terrain slanted and led to a river.

The same river where Brian's wife had died.

A cluster of footprints marred the freshly fallen snow and led to a treacherous path along the ice. A hole in the middle of the frozen stream made his gut tense.

"Help!"

He whipped his gaze downstream and the tinny taste of fear flooded his mouth. A hand shot through the ice, reaching skyward. Zoe's head bobbed up before she slipped and went back under, her fingers clawing to keep hold of the slick surface. Brian was nowhere to be found.

Staying on the narrow strip of land where the earth stopped and the river began, he sprinted toward her. "I'm coming Zoe," he yelled. "Just hold on. Please. Hold on."

He tossed his gun on the ground, shed his jacket, and kicked off his boots before dropping to his knees and flattening himself onto his stomach. Cracks splintered the thin ice, but the only chance Zoe had was him getting to her and pulling her to safety. He had to spread out his body weight as much as possible and inch his way toward her.

Blistering cold seeped through his shirt and torched his chest. Moisture dampened his jeans, and every slow movement he made in Zoe's direction was pure torture. He wanted to run to her, swoop her into his arms, and make her warm and safe. But that wasn't an option.

Her head poked through the hole again, and she gulped in a large breath. Her lips were blue and her eyes wide. "Cruz! Help me!"

"I'm right here, honey. I'm coming. I promise I won't let anything happen to you, okay? Do you trust me?"

Teeth chattering, she nodded.

"Just keep looking at me. Focus on my voice." He slid forward, closer and closer until the tips of his outstretched hand touched hers. Terror tightened his throat, but he couldn't think about everything he'd lose if he couldn't get to Zoe. Couldn't let it paralyze him. Not again.

A loud crack sounded and the hole widened, separating the sheet of ice Zoe clung to. She flailed, her arms shooting upward as her body sank into the frigid water, only her fingers visible, gripping the edge of the ice.

Cruz catapulted himself forward and plunged his arm into the river. The water hit his skin like a million pinpricks. He secured his throbbing hand around Zoe's forearm. Gritting his teeth, he pulled her toward him. She broke through the surface, gasping for air. Using his free hand, he grabbed her arm and hauled her over the tenuous ice. "We have to move. Have to get back to shore. The ice is thin so stay on your belly and move slowly."

"I...I can't move. Too cold." Her chin trembled, and her teeth chattered.

He cupped her cheek in his palm and locked his eyes with her. "You're Zoe Peyton. Soldier. Survivor. You're a badass woman who can do whatever she puts her mind to. And right now, I need you to move off the ice before we both fall in."

She set her shivering shoulders and locked her jaw.

Doing as he'd instructed, she slithered over the ice toward shore. He waited for her to pass him, not wanting too much weight concentrated on one spot, then followed behind.

Brooke emerged from the trees, her weapon still in her hand. "Oh my God! Are you two all right?"

"We will be," he called out. "Almost there, baby. Nice and slow. Keep moving."

Zoe reached the edge of the river and crawled onto the shore.

The ball of anxiety in his stomach melted, and he rushed to her side. "We need to get some of these wet clothes off you." The puffy, black coat clung to her, and he helped her out of it before discreetly doing the same with her sweater then huddling her into his discarded coat. She needed much more than a dry jacket to make sure she didn't get hypothermia, but this was all he could do for her now. He wrapped his arms around her, and a warmth he didn't think possible erupted inside him. She was safe and she was in his arms.

Finally.

"Well look at that. The gang's all here." Brian stepped out from around a tree with a gun pointed at the back of Brooke's head. "Don't even think about moving, or I'll put a bullet in this one's head."

Brooke stiffened.

Shit. He'd been so focused on saving Zoe, he hadn't stopped to wonder where Brian disappeared to. Brooke was a trained officer, and a damned good one at that, but she had no options against a man with a gun to her head.

"Zoe," Brian sang her name, drawing out each syllable. "Be a good girl and come here before I do something we both regret."

Cruz tightened his grip, refusing to let her move.

Shifting, she stared up at him. Eyes wide and lips quivering. "He'll kill her. You have to let me go," she whispered.

"No. I can't lose you." His voice cracked as his mind went into overdrive. Once Brian had Zoe, he'd kill both him and Brooke. Zoe giving him what he wanted wouldn't save anyone.

Brian took a step closer to Brooke, the end of his weapon now inches away from the crown of her head. "Stop. Talking. I'll give you five seconds before I lose my patience. One. Two."

Zoe pushed against Cruz. "I have to save her. Let me go."

Horror constricted his windpipe. He couldn't lose Zoe, but he couldn't sit back and watch Brooke be killed.

"Three," Brian yelled.

Brooke closed her eyes and jutted up her chin.

"Cruz. Please. Let me go."

"I can't. I love you, Zoe." Emotions boiled over, misting in his eyes. This wasn't how he wanted to tell her. With a madman pointing a gun at her best friend and all their lives in the balance. But he had to say it. Couldn't let her think for one more second that he didn't love her more than anything else on earth.

Zoe gasped then pressed her lips against his, knocking him off balance. She stumbled forward.

"Zoe!"

She glanced over her shoulder and mouthed, "I love you, too." She shoved her hands in the pocket of his jacket that still clung to her shoulders and hustled to Brooke's side. "Let them leave, and I'll do whatever you want."

Brian sneered and snatched her arm, yanking her in front of him. "Your friend needs to drop her weapon and walk away slowly."

Brooke dropped her gun and took a slow step.

Brian kept his gun trained on Brooke and snagged an arm around Zoe's waist.

Cruz kept his focus on Zoe. His gun still lay on the riverbank, mere feet away. But he'd never be able to get to it before Brian pulled the trigger. Helplessness vibrated his core, and a scream of rage built in his throat. He had to act, had to do something to keep them alive until Lincoln came with backup.

Zoe's body shook, and she huddled deeper into his coat. She plunged her hands into the pockets and her gaze flew to his. Determination stiffened her neck.

Anxiety sat heavy in his gut. He knew that look. *Damnit, Zoe, what's going on in your head?*

She dipped her chin and raised her brows as she leaned against Brian's arms, swaying a little to the side. "I'm s-sorry. I'm so cold." She bent her knees as if she were about to pass out.

Cruz shifted to the balls of his feet, ready to spring. Brooke took one more step forward then stopped as if sensing something was about to happen.

Brian pivoted, using his side to prop up Zoe. His arm went wide, the gun now pointed to the side.

Zoe yanked her fist from the coat pocket, the jagged ends of his keys nestled between her knuckles. She pulled back her arm and slammed her fist into Brian's face.

"Sonofa—" Brian stumbled backward and cradled his bloody cheek in his hand.

Zoe lunged to the side.

Cruz charged, blurring past Brooke and wrapping his arms around Brian's waist. He rammed his shoulder against the bastard as he drove him onto the cold ground. Anger pulsed in his veins, and he wanted nothing more than to pummel Brian's face.

Brian grunted and writhed beneath him, blood flowing from the gashes on his cheeks.

"Get the gun!" Brooke yelled.

Zoe smashed her foot down on Brian's wrist until his palm opened and released the weapon. She scooped it from the ground and pointed it at Brian. Her hands shook and her face was an alarming shade of white.

Cruz flipped Brian to his stomach and shoved his knee between his shoulder blades to keep him planted.

Brooke hurried over with a pair of cuffs and slapped them on Brian's wrists as the sound of footsteps crunched toward them.

"Pine Valley, PD," Lincoln called.

Relief flooded Cruz's system, and he jumped to his feet then hoisted Brian to his. Backup was here. Finally. "Took you long enough."

Lincoln snorted then slowed his gait as he approached, concern rippled across his forehead. "Next time don't bring me to the middle of nowhere. Everyone okay?" He flicked a glance at Brooke, then Zoe.

Cruz shoved Brian toward Lincoln, who snagged the man by the shirt then spun him around to grab the cuffs. Cruz gathered Zoe in his arms. He rubbed his hands up and down her body, trying to build up as much body heat as possible. "Zoe needs a medic. Now."

"One's in the driveway. Let's go."

Cruz swept Zoe into his arms, holding her against his chest, one arm under her knees and the other cradling her back.

Sighing, Zoe circled her arms around his neck and relaxed her head on his shoulder. Her breathing was slow... too slow. Her body temperature was low. A different kind of fear gripped his heart. Brian might not be a threat anymore, but Zoe wasn't out of the woods yet.

"Cruz?" She didn't lift her head as she spoke.

He ran as fast as he could, alarm ripping through him. "Yes?"

"Did you mean what you said? Do you love me?"

"With my whole damn heart, Zoe."

"I'm glad I got to hear that. I love you, too. I'm so cold. I just want to sleep. Is that okay?"

He pushed himself harder, faster. He had to keep her awake. Keep her talking. "Not yet, love. Let's talk about our future. What do you see?"

"Hmm." The sound hummed, but no words came out.

"I see a cabin in the woods," he said. "One with an amazing view of the mountains." Tears clogged his throat, but he had to keep talking. Keep her engaged.

"What else?"

"I see us sitting on the porch. Drinking wine while we rock in matching chairs, hand in hand. A yard full of kids running around. A little girl with your long legs and auburn hair. And a boy, too. Too bad he'll look like Lincoln." A chuckle broke through the mounting tears building against his eyes. "And a dog. I've always wanted a dog."

"Nice picture. Can't ever happen." Her head lolled to the side and her eyes slid shut.

His heart crumbled, but he kept running through the frozen forest until a clearing came into view. Red and blue lights slashed through the darkening sky. He raced for the ambulance, and an EMT rushed toward him. "She's at risk for hypothermia. She needs a warming blanket and fluids. She was in the ice. In the water. Her pulse is weak. Help her. Please. I can't lose her."

24

A bone-deep chill had Zoe pulling her favorite cashmere blanket tighter around her shoulders. A fire crackled in her fireplace, and Wyatt laid on the couch beside her with his head in her lap. She ran her fingers through the tuft of fur at the top of his fluffy head, losing her thoughts as she watched the flames dance on top of the stacked logs. Mere hours before, she was certain she was about to die. Now, as she sat safe and sound in her home with her best friend and a shattered heart, she almost wished she had.

Tears filled her eyes as the vision Cruz had explained for their future crushed her soul. A beautiful home they could share. A home filled with so much love. A home filled with children—their children—who looked like them.

Her chest tightened, and she allowed herself one more minute to grieve the loss of a future the man she loved had offered her. A future she could never have.

Brooke settled on the opposite side of the couch with two filled mugs, hot steam billowing into the air. "Drink this. It will help keep you warm."

Sniffing, Zoe grimaced. "I don't want any more tea. They made me drink enough of it at the hospital before they let me come home."

"Good thing it's not tea, then," Brooke said with a wink. "Hot chocolate with a shot of Bailey's. Whipped cream on top."

Zoe managed a small smile before taking the mug and forcing one sip. Her stomach soured, and she placed it on the stand beside her. "Thanks."

Brooke frowned and set down her own mug before sliding an arm around Zoe's shoulder and pulling her close, scooting a disgruntled Wyatt to the floor. "I know tonight was terrifying, but you're safe now. Brian can never hurt you again. Lincoln texted me while I was in the kitchen, and he and Cruz just finished their paperwork. Brian is locked up tight."

Cruz had stayed by Zoe's side while the emergency doctors had checked her over. As much as she hated being away from him, once he left for the station, she allowed herself to let down her walls and breathe. She might have professed her love to him, and he to her, but that didn't mean they could be together. That she could give him the life he wanted. Hell, the life she wanted. "You should go home," she said. "Be with Lincoln. I'm fine."

"You don't need to be alone right now. I can sleep on the couch."

Her friend's devotion chased away a little of the internal chill she couldn't shake, but as much as she loved Brooke, she *wanted* to be alone. Wanted to cry and wallow and be pissed as hell at the hand she'd been dealt.

A hard knock had Wyatt jumping to his feet and running to the door, fur lifted and barking.

Brooke motioned for Zoe to stay seated. "I got it."

Tensing, Zoe held her breath. She didn't need Brooke to open the door to know who stood on the other side.

Brooke glanced out the window before opening the door, and Cruz stepped through the threshold. Wyatt jumped, tail now wagging, but Cruz brushed him aside and hurried to Zoe. Concern and fatigue fought for top-billing in his deep-blue eyes. "How are you feeling?"

Shrugging, she offered a tentative smile. Dread slowed her heartrate. She didn't want to have this conversation right now, but there was no use putting it off. "I'm okay."

"I think I might take off after all," Brooke said, grabbing her coat from the hook. "Just call if you need anything. I can bring all the essentials for an old-fashioned slumber party and come back over anytime."

"Thanks."

Cruz crossed back to the door, locking the new deadbolt before taking the spot beside Zoe and pulling her against him. "Being away from you was torture."

She melted into him, inhaling the intoxicating scent of sandalwood and citrus that somehow clung to Cruz even after he'd shed his wet clothes and changed into spare scrubs at the hospital. "How are you?"

"Better now." He snuggled against her, dropping his lips to her forehead. "Brian confessed to everything. Even being responsible for the death of his wife. She was going to leave him, and he refused to let her go. He cornered her on the ice after he threatened to kill her, knowing she'd fall through. He would have gotten away with murder if he'd been able to let go of his anger toward her."

She shuddered. "So what? He used other women to take out his anger for the wife he killed?"

"Pretty much. You look a lot like her," Cruz said. "Like Brian's wife. He targeted women that reminded him of her, then used Leo to get close to them. Gain access. Made himself believe that you loved him then would leave him, so he needed to punish you."

"Oh my God." She squeezed her eyes shut as revulsion ripped through her. "Poor Leo. Poor Sandra. What does this mean for them?"

He skimmed his knuckles up and down her arm. "It means they are innocent victims caught in a sick game. I'll touch base with Sandra again tomorrow to give her some resources to help her and Leo get through this. But now, I just want to forget about this whole mess. At least for the rest of the night. I just want to be with you."

She stiffened then pulled away. The mug Brooke had given her still sat on the stand, and she debated chugging the hot liquid and hoping the Bailey's gave her the courage she needed to push through this conversation. Instead, she clasped her hands together in her lap, dancing her gaze anywhere in the room besides the beautiful man in front of her who held her heart. "You saved my life. I'll never be able to explain how grateful I am. I owe you the world for being there today."

Cruz's dark brows snapped together. "Zoe, I lost my mind when we didn't know where you were. I thought I'd never get a chance to tell you I love you. I'm sorry I was an idiot and couldn't explain how I was feeling after we slept together, but I'll never make that mistake again. You owe me nothing."

She cleared her suddenly dry throat and her heart slammed against her breastbone. "I owe you the truth. The things you said to me earlier, about seeing our future. It was all so beautiful, but it can never happen."

"What do you mean?"

She blew out a shaky breath. "I can't give you want you

want. I can't give you that beautiful picture you painted with the cabin and the kids. I can't be the woman you need. My friendship is all I have to offer." A pit of despair opened inside her, swallowing every dream she ever dared to hope. She didn't know how she'd go back to just being Cruz's friend, but she couldn't give him more than that.

Leaning forward, Cruz captured her hands in his. "You said you loved me too. Why can't we be together?" Confusion narrowed his eyes and he searched her gaze, looking for the answers she dreaded telling him.

She slid her fingers from under his and pressed her palms against her stomach. "We could never have that cabin in the woods with the kids running around. With the girl who looks like me and the little boy like you. I can never have children." Emotion clogged her throat and tears spilled over her lashes, trailing down her cheeks. Of all the things taken away from her in her lifetime, this was the worst. Not just the inability to carry Cruz's children, but to live a full life with the man she loved.

Cruz cradled her jawline in his hand and wiped away her tears with the pad of his thumb. "Honey, I don't need you to bear my children. I just need you."

She shook her head, not believing him. "You say that now, but you don't mean it. I can't jump into a relationship knowing I can't give you everything you deserve. Everything you've ever wanted. I'm not enough." A sob broke free, and she choked it back.

"Zoe, you are more than enough." Cruz's voice cracked. "You are everything. More than everything. A life with you —only you—is a life better than anything I could ever imagine. We could build a home and a family any way we want, however it looks. Adopted kids. No kids. Cats. Hell, I'll buy you a damn donkey if it'll make you happy. But *you* are my home. I want *you* to be my family."

Every ounce of her soul wanted to believe him, but she couldn't risk it. If he changed his mind and left her one day, she'd never recover. "You've always wanted a family of your own, Cruz. We both know it. You even planned to have one with Diana one day. Fate ripped that away from you once. I can't take it away from you again. I love you too much."

The side of Cruz's mouth hitched up. "Did I ever tell you Diana was adopted?"

She reared her head back and sniffed, trying to regain her composure. "You never mentioned that."

Sighing, Cruz rubbed a hand over his face. "I haven't opened up about my relationship with Diana like I should have. Not with you. Not with anyone. For so long, I blamed myself for her death. I should have reacted quicker during the robbery. Intervened and protected her. The fact that I stood and watched her be shot—watched her die—made me build so many walls. Walls to keep you out. Walls to keep all my guilt and self-doubt in. That wasn't fair to the memories and love I had for her, and it wasn't fair to you. I've loved you for so long but was too afraid to tell you. Too afraid I'd be the reason you were hurt one day. But all I did was waste time. I don't want to waste time anymore."

His declaration squeezed her heart, but it didn't change anything. "I'm glad you've lowered your walls, but I still can't give you the future you want."

He grinned. "I wasn't done. Diana was adopted, so when we planned our future, we decided we'd adopt as well. We wanted to foster children who need a home. Adopt a baby who didn't have parents to love them."

She swallowed a sigh. Although his heart was in the right place, she didn't need another person telling her she had options. That her inability to carry a child was just something for her to get over.

"But, baby, I want you to understand, I'm open to *any* future. As long as you're a part of it. So tell me, Zoe. What do you want?"

"I want you. But I'm so scared. Scared you'll change your mind. Or you'll see me as less. Or I don't know." She threw up her hands in frustration, unable to find the words to explain the turmoil she'd battled for so long. "I want to give you children. It breaks my heart that I can't."

He slid his hand down her jawline and cupped her chin between his thumb and forefinger. "Then we'll grieve that loss together. And then we'll find a way to move forward. A way that gives us both what we want. Just let me love you."

A dam burst open and she threw her arms around him, burying her face in his neck. She'd spent so many years afraid of what her inability to have children meant for her future. She'd never taken the time to mourn that loss. Now here was a man who not only loved her and wanted a future with her, he wanted to grieve with her.

And then they could stand together, picking each other up, and build something wonderful and perfect that she never imagined could be her reality.

Shifting, she faced him. Studied the kind eyes and new scruff that added an edge she loved. She framed his face in her hands, studying every feature. Every line. "Are you sure?"

Grinning, he rolled his eyes. "Damnit, what else do I have to say?"

"Say you love me." She smiled, her heart melting at this man who meant everything to her.

His grin faded and a seriousness she seldom saw took

over his expression. "I love you, Zoe Peyton. I love *all* of you."

"I love you, too, Cruz." She pressed her lips to his, sinking into the feel of him. The taste of him. And the core of her knew, Cruz would always be home. He'd always be her family. And they'd build that picture into whatever they wanted, for many years to come.

EPILOGUE

Pops of yellow and hues of purple exploded along the dirt path that wound through the vibrant green grass. Zoe linked her hand in Cruz's as they meandered along the trail between the towering maple trees. It wasn't often they both had a full day off together, and she planned to enjoy every single minute.

Not like she hadn't enjoyed every minute of the past few months. Days spent getting to know Cruz on a deeper level than ever before. Nights spent in his arms, being showered with love and cared for by his tender—and talented—hands. Even when the nightmares came, or the bouts of panic triggered by a smell or a sound paralyzed her, Cruz was right there, helping her navigate her trauma.

Water gurgled somewhere in the distance, and she shuddered.

Cruz squeezed her hand, lines creasing his furrowed brow. "Are you okay?"

She nodded. "Yes. It's just the water." Stopping, she glanced around. A clearing gave way to an open piece of land. Beams of warm sunlight spotlighted the area, and she turned questioning eyes to Cruz. "Where are we?"

Smirking, he shrugged and tugged her forward. He dipped his head, indicating the mountain range rising to meet the blue sky. "What do you think of the view?"

"It's beautiful. I've never been on this trail before. Are we still in the state park?" She roamed her gaze over the peaks and valleys spread out before her, then tried to find the trail that seemed to end when they got to the clearing.

"I found this spot right after we started dating. I've looked into the property, and the owner is an old man in town who'd like to sell. The price is right, and I think now's the time to start building that future."

Tilting her head, she crinkled her brow and tried to decipher his words. "What do you mean?"

He waved an arm in the air as if offering her the world. "Our cabin in the woods. We could build the porch here, facing the mountains. We could sit hand in hand, sipping wine while we watch the sunset every night. What do you say?"

Joy radiated through her. "You want to live together?"

He nodded. "Only if you're ready."

She fisted a hand on her hip. "What about that donkey you said you'd buy me?"

A deep laugh rolled through him. "It's still on the table, if you want it, but I had something else in mind." He stuck his fingers in his mouth and let out a shrill whistle.

A light brown furball with wrinkles creasing every surface of its skin and tiny ears ran out from behind a tree. Lincoln grinned from beside the tree, waving before quietly retreating in the opposite direction.

"Oh my gosh! How cute." Zoe knelt down and scooped

the furball into her arms before standing again and facing Cruz. "Is he ours?"

Cruz grinned. "She. And yes. If you want her."

Zoe pressed her forehead to the puppy, who licked at her face. "What's her name?"

"Jasmine." Cruz scrunched up his nose. "But she's a shar pei mixed with a pit bull so I don't think she'll be a dainty little flower. She needs a beefier name."

Zoe laughed. "Beefy?"

Cruz shrugged.

Inspiration struck Zoe. "What about Bacchus?"

"Say what?"

"Bacchus. The Roman God of wine. You know, like all those nights we'll spend on the porch, sipping wine, living every day together in love and laughter." She squeezed the dog tight, and the pup's butt wiggled. "It's a little unconventional, but that's why it's perfect. Like us."

Cruz wrapped an arm around her shoulders, and Bacchus leapt toward him, kissing his face while Zoe fought to keep her in her arms. "I think she likes it. Our family, growing the way we want it, with a brand-new home and a little fur baby."

Zoe kissed his cheek then stared at the view she hoped to see for the next fifty years. With the man she loved—and whoever else they gathered into their fold—by her side.

Their home. Their family. Their forever.

DON'T MISS out on Chet and Mia's story in Crossroads of Redemption. Chet's walls are forced down after Mia finds a body with a wrist singed with the same markings burned

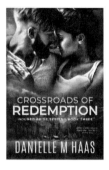

into his own flesh—given by the man who killed his wife and child. But when a killer returns, more than one life is on the line.

ACKNOWLEDGMENTS

I wanted to take a moment and thank all the people in my life who have lifted me up when I've needed it throughout this remarkable journey. My husband and children have allowed me to shut myself away in my office for hours while I met deadlines and tried to wrap my mind around marketing. My parents and sister have given me so much of their time while I've plotted and complained and asked for validation. My Haas' Hustlers have left encouraging words and exciting reviews that make me feel like I'm doing something right.

Thank you to Kate Scholl, my editor who made this book what it is, and the amazing designers at Deranged Doctors who created the most beautiful covers. Thanks to Melinda Crown for searching out those pesky typos for me! So much appreciate for my critique partners, Julie Anne Lindsey and Samantha Wilde, you both are my backbone in this industry.

And most of all to the readers! It amazes me every day that you chose to read my book. I appreciate you and love you all!

Until we meet again,
    Danielle M Haas

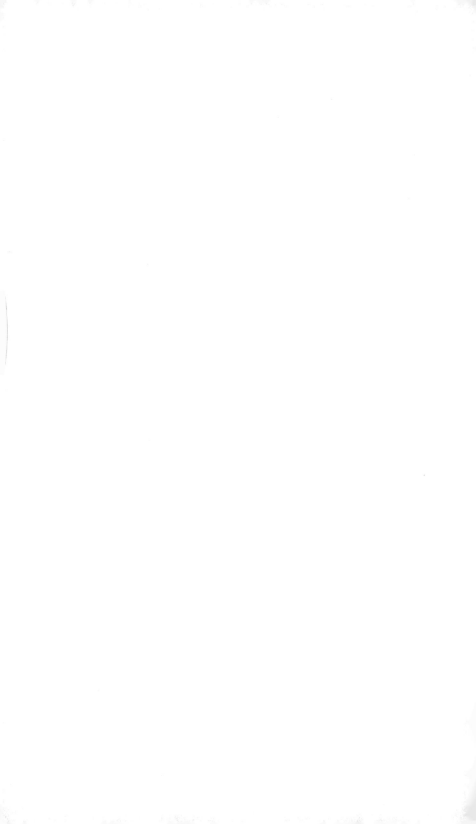

ABOUT THE AUTHOR

Danielle grew up with a love of reading, partly due to her namesake—Danielle Steele. It seemed as though she was born to write out the same love stories she devoured while growing up.

She attended Bowling Green State University with a dream of studying creative writing, but the thought of sharing her work in front of a group of strangers was enough to make her change her major to Political Science.

After college she moved across the state of Ohio with her soon-to-be husband. Once they married and had babies, she decided to stay home and raise her children. Some days her sanity slipped further across the line to crazy town so she decided to brush off her rusty writing chops and see what happened.

Danielle now spends her days running kids around, playing with her beloved dog, and typing as fast as she can to get the stories in her head written down. She loves to write contemporary romance with relatable characters that make her readers' hearts happy, as well as fast-paced romantic suspense that leaves them on the edge of their seats. Her story ideas are as varied and unpredictable as her everyday life.

ALSO BY DANIELLE M HAAS

Injured Pride Series

Crossroads of Revival

Crossroads of Revenge

Murders of Convenience Series

Matched with Murder

Booked to Kill

Driven to Kill

The Sheffield Series

Second Time Around

A Place In This World

Coming Home

Stand Alones

Bound by Danger

Girl Long Gone